For Blood and Wine are Red

By the same author

And Death The Prize
Death in the Skies

For Blood and Wine are Red

RICHARD GRAYSON

ROBERT HALE · LONDON

First published in Great Britain 2000

ISBN 0 7090 6679 1

Robert Hale Limited
Clerkenwell House
Clerkenwell Green
London EC1R 0HT

2 4 6 8 10 9 7 5 3 1

Typeset by
Derek Doyle & Associates, Liverpool.
Printed in Great Britain by
St Edmundsbury Press, Bury St Edmunds, Suffolk.

For blood and wine are red
And blood and wine were on his hands
When they found him with the dead.

Oscar Wilde
The Ballad of Reading Gaol

For Blood and Wine are Red

1

Along each side of the great hall of the Château Perdrix banners hung down from the raftered roof, some bearing the coats of arms of the oldest families of Burgundy, others painted with the heraldic devices adopted by the wine-growing châteaux. Below on the long oak refectory tables which had been set out in rows over the full length of the hall, stood silver goblets, jugs and platters, each with some historical significance in the viticulture of the region. On a stage that had been erected at one end of the hall six empty velvet thrones had been placed in a semicircle, waiting for those who were that evening to be invested with the order of *La Confrérie des Chevaliers du Tastevin de Bourgogne*. Behind the thrones hung more banners, each representing the principal châteaux of the region which had joined forces to create the new order.

The three hundred guests invited to this, the inaugural meeting of the *Confrérie*, had just finished a banquet of eleven courses. With each course one of the best known wines of the region had been served. As the guests tasted the wines, the Grand Sommelier of the new order, speaking from the stage, had explained the merits and particular attributes of them. Now the dinner and the *dégustation* were over and presently the *intronisation* of the new Chevaliers was to begin.

The chair to Gautier's left was vacant. He had been invited to attend the banquet and induction ceremony that evening by Duthrey, whom he had known for many years. A journalist on the staff of *Le Figaro* in Paris, Duthrey had been selected as one of the six men who were to be admitted to the *Confrérie* that evening. It was a great honour, he had assured Gautier, for the other initiates were well-known figures in the wine trade, all proprietors of vineyards producing internationally recognized *grand cru* wines. Duthrey had been chosen on account of a book which he had recently written on the wines of Burgundy and which was selling well all over France.

In spite of his often testy manner and dogmatic opinions, Duthrey was by nature shy and he had felt he would need the support of a friend at the ordeal he would have to endure that evening at a ceremony to be held before more than three hundred people. So he had persuaded Gautier to accompany him. They had travelled down from Paris that morning and would spend the night at a hotel in Dijon before returning home the following day. Now he had left his seat at the banquet to join the other initiates at the back of the hall, from where they would be led in procession up on to the stage.

Gautier knew little about the new *Confrérie*, which he was inclined to see as no more than another example of the French passion for decorations. Best known of the honours which could be bestowed on French men and women was of course the Légion d'honneur, which had been created by Napoleon a little more than a century previously. Since that time more than fifty thousand people in all had been invested with one or other of the Légion's ranks: chevaliers, officiers, commandeurs, grand officiers – and more were being accorded the honour every year for their services to the country. There were several other similar though lesser awards, reserved for people in different occupations: agriculture, schoolteaching, municipal police, customs and excise and the postal services. Even porters in Les Halles, the markets of Paris, had their own decoration.

The *Confrérie* was a new and relatively minor order, but even so that evening Gautier was impressed with the trouble that its sponsors had taken to invest its inaugural meeting with dignity and style. The man sitting on his right, with whom he had exchanged a few words during the banquet and whose name was Pascal, obviously agreed for he suddenly remarked, 'You are fortunate to be here, my friend. This evening may well mark the beginning of a new age for the wines of Burgundy.'

'In what way?'

'Time will show that the founding of the *Confrérie* was a great step forward.'

'What is the purpose behind it, may I ask?'

'It will have two main objectives,' Pascal replied. 'One will be to maintain and improve the quality of the wines produced in the region.'

'How will this be done?'

'By controlling the yield from every hectare of grapes in a vineyard and laying down the minimum and maximum limits of alcoholic strength for the wine. The details are being worked out and in due course they will be embodied in a charter.'

'And the second objective?'

'To enhance and spread the reputation of wines from Burgundy until they carry the same prestige as Bordeaux wines.'

Gautier was aware that for centuries wines from Bordeaux had possessed a special cachet outside France, not only the *grands crus classés* wines from Paulliac and Margaux, the 'clarets' as the English called them, but also Graves, Sauternes and other sweet wines. Shippers of Bordeaux wines had a thriving export business with England which dated back to the middle ages, when the south-west of France belonged to the English crown.

'And you believe that these objectives can be achieved?' Gautier asked Pascal.

'I am convinced of it, although there are some in the wine business who believe that the sponsors of the *Confrérie* have acted too hastily. They say we are trying to run before we can walk and that in ten, maybe twenty years, we will be ready for a *Confrérie*.'

Pascal, who was a talkative fellow, was clearly ready to expand on his reasons for supporting the creation of the *Confrérie*. He was prevented from doing so, for at that moment they heard the sound of horns coming from the back of the hall, a signal that the ritual of the *intronisation* was about to begin.

They looked round and saw that two trumpeters were leading a procession up the centre of the hall. Behind them came three men dressed in scarlet robes not unlike those worn a century or two ago by doctors of law, with gold sashes over their shoulders. The scarlet hats they were wearing also had a vaguely academic look. Gautier supposed that they must be officers of the new *Confrérie*, the Grand Officier perhaps and his two deputies. They were followed by the six men who were to be made Chevaliers that evening, walking in couples, also wearing similar robes, but without sashes and bareheaded. As the procession passed Gautier, Duthrey, who was one of the six, did not look round at him, but stared straight ahead to conceal his self-consciousness.

The procession filed up the stairs leading to the stage, where the trumpeters separated to take up their positions, one on each side. The six neophytes were then led in turn to one of the thrones where they were left standing, facing the spectators, waiting for their initiation into the *Confrérie*. Returning to the front of the stage, the Grand Officier of the *Confrérie* then gave an address in Latin, reading from a vellum scroll which was handed to him by one of his aides.

Gautier had only a rudimentary knowledge of Latin, but he gathered that the theme of the address was to remind all those present of the traditions of winemaking in Burgundy and of the determination of the *Confrérie* that these should be maintained. When the Grand Officier had finished his address, he and the other two officers began going round in turn to all the six neophytes standing in front of their thrones. Each of them was asked three questions, also in Latin, to which they responded. Gautier guessed they were being asked to confirm their loyalty to the *Confrérie* and its code of conduct. Then each of them was tapped by the Grand Officier on both shoulders with a wooden staff made from the stalk of a vine. Finally each man sat down in his throne and the Grand Officier placed around his shoulders a golden ribbon at the end of which hung a silver medal. As this was being done the trumpeters played a clarion call.

Only three of the six neophytes had been admitted as Chevaliers of the *Confrérie*, when the ceremony was interrupted by a commotion and shouting from the far end of the hall. Looking round Gautier saw a man in a grey suit wearing a clerical collar, shrugging off two attendants who were trying to stop him entering. He came striding up the aisle between the tables, heading for the stage.

'Stop this!' he was shouting in English. 'In the name of the Lord and of Christianity I order you to stop this!'

Everyone in the hall stared at the man, astonished by his behaviour and by the aggression in his language. No one attempted to stop him as he strode towards the stage and climbed the steps leading up to it. Gautier saw that he was carrying what looked like a stick, but as soon as he was on the stage, he released the thong, showing that it was a whip. He turned to face the spectators.

'You who sell drink sell sin,' he shouted. 'Alcohol is the fount of sin, of fornication and adultery, of impiety and deceit and every abomination. Just as Christ cleared the temple, I shall clear this house and drive out the peddlers of sin.'

He began cracking his whip, aiming not at anyone in particular but in the general direction of the hall and the spectators. The two attendants who had followed him were standing at the foot of the steps leading up to the stage, listening to the man and not knowing what they should do. The Grand Officier went to the edge of the stage and beckoned to them.

'Take this gentleman away,' he told them. 'Use as much force as you need.'

The attendants climbed up on to the stage, nervously it seemed to Gautier, afraid that the man might lash out at them with his whip. Instead he stopped his whipping and dropped his arms to his sides, as though ready to be taken prisoner. The attendants seized him, hustled him down the steps and began marching him towards the exit of the hall. As they went the man continued shouting, calling on God to destroy all who sold drink, then urging the makers of wine to repent, to stop their evil trade and seek salvation.

'Who is that man?' Gautier asked Pascal. 'Have you ever seen him before?'

'As it happens I have. He is a Methodist bishop, the leader of a political movement in America. He was speaking at a public meeting in Dijon only this morning.'

'What have American politics to do with France?'

Pascal shrugged. 'If you ask me he is a little mad.'

'Is he violent?'

'He could easily be.'

Gautier decided that he must act. Although as an Inspector of the Sûreté in Paris he had no standing in local matters of law and order, he felt that the two attendants might welcome the assistance of authority and as far as he knew there were no policemen present at the Château Perdrix that evening. He also felt he had a duty to make sure that his friend Duthrey's *intronisation* should not suffer any further disruptions. Leaving the table he walked down towards the end of the hall. There by the entrance to the building he found the bishop still held prisoner by the attendants. He was no longer shouting, but still protesting.

'You have no right to do this!' he told the two men, speaking French now, although badly and with an atrocious accent.

'Monsieur le Curé,' one of the men said persuasively. 'You have had your fun. Why don't you go away now, there's a good fellow?'

Learning that he had been mistaken for a mere parish priest did not displease the bishop as much as one might have expected. Gautier had formed the impression that he would not be deflected from his purpose that evening by any trifling discourtesies.

'I insist that you release me and allow me to go back and address the people in the hall,' he told the two men. 'I have a right to be heard.'

'Monsieur,' Gautier asked him firmly, 'do you have an invitation to this meeting? If so, show it to us.'

'I need no invitation. I am speaking in the name of the Lord.'

'If you persist in this behaviour, you will be arrested, taken to Dijon and thrown into jail.'

'And who are you, Monsieur? What authority do you have, may I ask?'

'I am an inspector with the Sûreté in Paris.'

One could sense a change in the bishop's attitude. He had been ready to bully the two attendants, but was not prepared to challenge the police.

'I have broken no law,' he said.

'How did you come to this hall?' Gautier asked him.

'I was driven here from Dijon by automobile.' The bishop

pointed towards where a small number of automobiles were parked among the carriages, which had brought most of the guests to the château that evening. Automobiles were commonplace in Paris now and there were increasing complaints in the city that they were disrupting the traffic in the streets, as well as threatening the lives of pedestrians. One might have supposed, though, that few would be found in Dijon.

'In that case I will escort you to your auto,' Gautier said firmly 'and you will return to Dijon.'

The bishop did not protest or argue. It may have been that he believed he had achieved his purpose in coming to the meeting that evening and was ready to leave. He led Gautier to the parked automobiles, in one of which a young man was sitting at the steering wheel.

The bishop pointed towards the man. 'This is Monsieur Fallière, who was kind enough to drive me out here from Dijon.'

Fallière was not dressed in any uniform, which suggested he was not a professional chauffeur, nor was he wearing the leather jacket, helmet or other accoutrements popular with amateur drivers. He had a notebook on his lap in which he had been writing.

Gautier introduced himself and then added, 'I understand, Monsieur, that you brought this gentleman here from Dijon.'

Fallière grinned insolently. 'Bishop Arkwright put on quite a show in there, did he not?' He inclined his head in the direction of the hall.

'How do you know?'

'I was watching from the back.'

'What is your interest in the proceedings?'

'I work on the staff of *Le Bien Public* in Dijon. I am a newspaper reporter.'

'Well, Monsieur, now perhaps you would be good enough to drive the bishop back to Dijon. He is not welcome here.'

*

'The evening – my evening – was ruined!' Duthrey said angrily.

'Let us not exaggerate, old friend. Apart from that childish display by the American bishop, the evening was a great success; an impressive ceremony conducted with style and taste.'

'It was a disaster!' Duthrey replied morosely.

'In no way. Most of the people in the hall would not have even heard what the man was saying. Others would have treated his intervention with scorn.'

Duthrey would not be consoled. 'The man should be arrested. Thrown in jail!'

The two of them were being driven back in a carriage provided by the *Confrérie* to the hotel where they were to spend the night. Gautier could understand Duthrey's indignation, but what he had said was true. The behaviour of Bishop Arkwright at the *intronisation* ceremony had been no more than an irritating diversion, a piece of comic relief in the evening which would soon be forgotten.

'What was the man trying to achieve?' Gautier asked. 'What were his motives for that extraordinary outburst?'

'Bishop Arkwright is one of the leaders of the Anti-Saloon League, a temperance movement in America. His arrival in France a few days ago was reported in my paper. The objective of the League is to promote total abstinence, to stop people drinking.'

'Stop drinking? How?'

'The temperance movement has a great deal of influence in the United States. Its leaders are confident that within a short time Congress will pass a law prohibiting the sale of all alcoholic drinks. Now they hope to spread their pernicious creed in our country.'

Gautier laughed. 'Stop Frenchmen drinking? They cannot be

serious! Are they not aware that wine is a part of life for us? Essential for the enjoyment of food, for appetite, for health?'

'They are fanatics, religious fanatics. The temperance movement was spawned in the Middle West of America, the so-called bible belt. It is dominated by the Nonconformist sects; Baptists, Methodists, Quakers.'

'You seem very well informed on the subject.'

'Some weeks ago *Figaro* asked me to write a series of articles on present-day comparative religions.'

They started talking about the religions of the world and their various sects. Thinking it would distract Duthrey and lessen his sense of grievance, Gautier led him on with questions. They were spending the night in Dijon at a small, elegant hotel called L'Hostellerie du Chapeau Rouge, which could trace its origins back to the fourteenth century and took its name from a cardinal's red hat. When they arrived there they went into a salon adjoining the vestibule and found a waiter who brought them a bottle of cognac.

While they were enjoying their *digestif* Duthrey showed Gautier what had been hung round his neck at the ceremony that evening to confirm his election as a Chevalier of the *Confrérie*. It was not, as Gautier had believed, a medal but a *tastevin*, the traditional cup of the wine-taster or *sommelier*. Beautifully fashioned in silver, its shape was not unlike that of a scallop-shell, flared to allow anyone examining a wine to nose it before tasting. Now Duthrey's lay in a small red presentation box which he had been given after the ceremony The top of the box was engraved with a crest, featuring a knight's casque and a harp.

As he closed the box Duthrey pointed to the crest. 'That is the family coat of arms of Michael O'Flynn, the Grand Officier of the *Confrérie*.'

'O'Flynn? That is not a French name, surely?'

'No, Irish. Michael is descended from an Irish officer who fought for Napoleon.'

Gautier remembered reading somewhere that a large number of Irishmen had fought in the French army during the eighteenth century. This had been at a time when English laws against Catholics made it impossible for young Irishmen to enter a profession or to have any other worthwhile career in their own country. With no prospects many of those who did not own land went to fight in Europe as soldiers of fortune. At the battle of Fonteney in 1745 there had been no fewer than six Irish regiments in the French army.

'Michael's ancestor, also Michael O'Flynn, left the army,' Duthrey explained, 'married into a French family and acquired a vineyard. Today his Château Perdrix produces one of the best red wines in Burgundy.'

Duthrey went on to say that it had been O'Flynn who was behind the formation of the *Confrérie*. He had persuaded the owners of the other leading vineyards in the region to become involved and had provided the funds needed to launch the new organization and for the initiation ceremony that evening, which had been held in a hall at his château.

From the room in which they were sitting they could see into the vestibule of the hotel. While they were talking Gautier noticed a man accompanied by a woman come in from the street and cross towards the reception desk. He had to look a second time before he realized that the man was Arkwright, the American bishop who had disrupted the *intronisation* earlier that evening. The woman accompanying him would not have been much younger than Arkwright, in her early forties perhaps, but she was handsome and dressed with style. At the desk the bishop was given a key and he and the woman began going up the staircase leading to the upper floors of the hotel. Gautier pointed the couple out to Duthrey.

'Are you saying that the man is staying here? In our hotel?' Duthrey exclaimed. 'That's monstrous!'

'Perhaps he has aspirations to becoming a cardinal.'

The joke was too subtle for Duthrey. 'Hardly. His Anti-Saloon League blames Catholics and immigrants from Europe for all the evils of life in America, for sin, corruption, prostitution, Catholics and of course the demon drink! The man should not have been allowed in this hotel.'

Gautier could understand Duthrey's indignation even though he did not share it. He was surprised that Arkwright should be staying at Le Chapeau Rouge, but for a different reason. He had always understood that the teachings of the Noncomformist sects of the Christian church were based on self-denial and an austere, parsimonious life. How could it be then, that a Methodist bishop was lodging in one of Dijon's most luxurious hotels?

'This bishop would be well advised to leave Dijon first thing in the morning,' Duthrey remarked.

'What makes you say that?'

'Although he restrained his anger at the time, O'Flynn was enraged by the man's behaviour. He thought, as I did, that the evening had been ruined and that he himself had been made to look foolish. He swore that he would make this bishop pay for his insolence. I would not rule out violence. One knows what fiery tempers the Irish have.'

Early next morning Gautier took a stroll through the streets of Dijon. As it was a Sunday there were few people to be seen, apart from four or five old ladies on their way to the nearby cathedral of St Bénigne for the first Mass of the day. Evidently all but the most disciplined of the city's Catholics preferred to leave their devotions to a more civilized hour. Gautier himself had found that he could no longer endure the luxury of rising late. At one time on Sunday mornings in Paris he would lie on in bed, enjoying the silence, the absence of early morning sounds coming up from the streets, the noise of cartwheels, the cries of tradesmen calling out to offer their produce to cooks and housewives. That had been years previously when he was married. Since then he had lost the habit and now, even on the infrequent occasions when one of his mistresses was spending the night at his home, he would rise early, begin tidying the apartment and making their *petit déjeuner*.

That morning when he had left it to come out into the streets, the hotel had been peaceful with only two cleaners at work downstairs and a night porter dozing in the hall. Duthrey no doubt would still have been in bed, for in Gautier's experience journalists, who frequently spent much of their nights chasing news or simply carousing, seldom enjoyed rising early. He walked for the best part of an hour through the narrow winding streets, admiring the sleepy charm of their old buildings. As he walked he found himself wondering what his life would be like if he lived and worked in Dijon instead of Paris. One might suppose that there would be relatively few crimes in the district beyond drunkenness, occasional petty fraud in the commercial quarter and domestic violence between man and wife or jealous lovers. In Paris he had been given a special responsibility for trying to protect the many thousands of British and American tourists who had been pouring into the city for the last few years, since the *Exposition Universelle* of 1900. Although foreign visitors were seldom involved in major crimes, looking after their welfare was time-consuming if not particularly onerous. Even so, he had the feeling that he was contented enough in Paris and might find life in Dijon tedious.

By the time he arrived back at L'Hostellerie du Chapeau Rouge, the hotel had come to life. Two carriages were drawn up in the street outside, the coachmen waiting, he assumed, for the hotel guests they had come to collect, and an automobile – a Panhard Levassor – was parked behind them. A policeman in uniform was standing at the entrance to the hotel and there were two more in the lobby. Policemen usually meant trouble. Gautier was curious to know why they were there, so he went up to one of them, and told him who he was and that he was staying at the hotel.

Then he asked him, 'Has there been some trouble here?'

'Yes, Monsieur l'Inspecteur. Not long ago a dead body was found upstairs in the first floor corridor.'

'A suicide?'

'No. Apparently the man had been stabbed.' The policeman looked at Gautier, wondering perhaps how much more he should tell him. Then he added, 'And there's another strange thing. The dead man was wearing a cardinal's hat.'

Gautier did not ask the man any more questions. The homicide was no affair of his and policemen were often jealous of anyone who might be seeming to interfere or to usurp their authority. So he moved away to the back of the lobby and waited. His first thought had been one of anxiety over Duthrey's safety, but common sense told him that his concern was needless. There could be no one in Dijon who might wish to harm Duthrey and in any case both Duthrey's room and his own were on the second floor of the hotel.

He waited in the lobby to see what would happen. Presently a police inspector came down the stairs. Behind him came two more policemen, one holding Bishop Arkwright by the arm and the other escorting the woman whom Gautier and Duthrey had seen entering the hotel with Arkwright the previous evening. Clearly they were being taken away by the police for questioning.

He crossed over to the hotel's reception desk and asked the

concierge who was standing behind it, 'Is it true that someone was stabbed to death in the hotel last night?'

'Yes, Monsieur. A shocking affair, shocking!'

'Do you know who the dead man was?'

'Yes, Monsieur. He was well known in Dijon, one might say a public figure. Michael O'Flynn owned one of the region's finest vineyards.'

2

Gautier knocked on the door of Duthrey's hotel room. He had decided that his friend should be told as soon as possible about the murder of Michael O'Flynn. The Dijon police would no doubt follow routine procedures in its investigations and all the guests in the hotel, as well as the staff, were likely to be questioned in the hope that they might have seen or heard something which could have a bearing on the murder. That would take time and as a result, it was possible that Duthrey and Gautier might be delayed in returning to Paris.

He went into the room and found Duthrey sitting up in bed, expecting, no doubt, that the knock on the door had been that of a maid bringing in his *petit déjeuner*. In addition to a long night-shirt to protect him from the chill of the night, he was wearing a nightcap, which, as soon as he saw Gautier, he quickly pulled off and stuffed under his pillow.

'What is it?' he asked sharply.

Gautier knew he must not allow himself to smile. Nightcaps had been worn by men in the last century, but times had changed and now they looked faintly ludicrous. Even night-shirts had become *passée*. Those men who wore anything in bed were beginning to favour pyjamas, a novel fashion which had reached England from the British colony of India. People had been suspicious of pyjamas at first, believing them to be unhygienic and even dangerous to health, but they were now being given a cautious acceptance. Duthrey was not one for daring experiments, but he might even so find it embarrassing were his friends to discover that he still slept as his grandfather had.

'I have bad news for you,' Gautier told him. 'Your friend Monsieur O'Flynn is dead.'

'Dead!' Duthrey stared at him in disbelief. 'What are you saying?'

'Unfortunately it is true. He was murdered last night.'

'Where?'

'Here in this hotel.'

Duthrey listened while Gautier told him what he had learned from the policeman. Then he said, 'That American, the bishop, must be responsible.'

'Why do you say that?'

'Can you not see?' Duthrey began to grow excited. 'Did I not tell you that O'Flynn was enraged by the man's insolence? He must have come to the hotel last night, they quarrelled and the American stabbed him.'

'The bishop and his lady-friend have been taken away by the police for questioning.'

'There you are then!'

Gautier was not convinced. Michael O'Flynn might well have come to the hotel to confront Arkwright, but he could not imagine that Arkwright would have stabbed him. He had formed the impression that the bishop was a political animal, a man consumed by a belief in his own importance, ready to threaten and bully, but not a man of violence. He remembered how, at the *intronisation* ceremony the previous evening, Arkwright had surrendered tamely when the two attendants had begun to remove him from the hall.

While they had been talking a maid had come into the room with Duthrey's breakfast. She was full of apologies for her tardiness in arriving and could barely restrain her excitement, the fearful excitement always aroused in people when they came into contact with a violent death. Leaving Duthrey to his breakfast, Gautier went to his own room, where he packed his valise, ready for the return to Paris. Then he went downstairs.

By now the hotel lobby was crowded. Guests who had come down from their bedrooms and been told of the murder that had been committed during the night, were talking excitedly among themselves. Their excitement was the same as that which Gautier had noticed in the maid who had brought Duthrey's breakfast to his room. The police had taken over the manager's office, where they were questioning all the hotel staff and the guests one by one to find out whether they knew anything which might be related to the murder. A small crowd of people had gathered in the street outside the hotel and one might expect that the crime would soon be a sensation in Dijon.

Gautier asked the concierge to have his valise brought down from his room and then went to the desk to settle his account. Duthrey had still not appeared, but Gautier was not surprised. A man who wore a night-cap was likely to be fastidious and painstaking with his toilet. While he was waiting he noticed a man walking across the lobby towards him. It took him a few seconds to recognize him as Armand Pascal, the man who had sat next to him at the *intronisation* ceremony the previous evening.

'Inspector Gautier,' Pascal shook him by the hand. 'What are you doing here?'

'Monsieur Duthrey and I spent last night in the hotel.'

'I thought perhaps that you might be involved in investigating the murder.'

'No. You have heard about it then?'

'The whole town is talking of nothing else. Shocking business is it not? Who on earth would wish to kill O'Flynn?'

'He was a popular man, was he?'

'Certainly. As I told you last evening not everyone supported the *Confrérie*, but O'Flynn was well liked in Dijon.'

They chatted for a time. Pascal told Gautier that he himself lived some twenty kilometres to the north, where he owned a vineyard. He had come into Dijon that morning for an appointment with two business associates who were arriving by train from Paris. They had arranged to meet at the Hostellerie du Chapeau Rouge.

'The police were reluctant to let me into the hotel when I arrived. They have orders to keep people away.'

'One can understand that. Inquisitive crowds would only hamper their investigation.'

'So they do not know who killed O'Flynn?'

'Evidently not.'

'Surely they must have suspects?'

Gautier shrugged. He could think of no comment that he could usefully make. All crimes, especially murder, must be treated objectively and their solution was not helped by idle speculation. Pascal however was not prepared to let the matter rest. He asked Gautier, 'Do you suppose that the murder might in some way be connected with that scene at the *intronisation* ceremony last night?'

'Anything is possible. I really do not know.'

'O'Flynn was furious at the American's behaviour. I have never seen him so angry.'

When he saw that Gautier would not be drawn, Pascal seemed to grow restless. He pulled out a silver watch from his waistcoat pocket and looked at it.

'I cannot imagine why my friends from Paris are not here yet,' he said. 'Their train from Paris must have been delayed.'

'Perhaps the police would not admit them to the hotel. They could be waiting outside.'

'You may be right. I will go and see.'

The number of people in the lobby showed no signs of diminishing. Gautier noticed one or two guests coming out of the manager's office, presumably having been questioned, they then left the hotel with their luggage, but progress was slow. Presently the inspector of police whom he had seen earlier leaving the hotel with Bishop Arkwright and his lady companion, returned alone and went into the manager's office. When finally Duthrey did appear, Gautier told him that they would both have to take their turn and be questioned by the police before they returned to Paris.

'Quite right too,' Duthrey said. 'I can tell them who murdered O'Flynn.'

'I would not be too ready with accusations if I were you.'

'Why not? The American bishop must have killed him.'

'You have no evidence that he was responsible.'

'Like all policemen you are too cautious,' Duthrey said. 'There is another reason for believing that the bishop is guilty. Did you not say that O'Flynn was found wearing a cardinal's hat?'

'Yes, but what is the connection?'

'Bishop Arkwright hated Catholics. He denounced the Catholic Church as the mother of superstition, bigotry and vice. After stabbing O'Flynn he must have put the hat on him as a gesture of defiance.'

Gautier could see little logic in Duthrey's reasoning. 'Leave matters to the police,' he advised him. 'If you start accusing the bishop you will be drawn into the investigation. And that may mean that you and I might have to stay on in Dijon. As it is we may well have to take a later train to Paris.'

The suggestion that they might be delayed in returning home did not disconcert Duthrey as much as Gautier had expected. In Paris after taking his daily apéritif at the Café Corneille, Duthrey would return home, where his wife had prepared an excellent lunch for him. The lunch would be accompanied by a bottle of burgundy, after which he would take a short nap before returning to the offices of *Le Figaro*. The daily routine had become a ritual, any breach of which invariably provoked a burst of petulance. Gautier had never met Madame Duthrey and knew only that they were an apparently devoted couple who had no children. He had assumed on little evidence that it must be Madame Duthrey who laid down the rules of their marriage and who expected punctuality of her husband. Now Duthrey seemed almost to welcome the possibility that he might be delayed in returning to the domestic milieu.

While they were talking a policeman came up and told them that Inspector Le Harivel would like to speak to them in the manager's office. When they were shown in, Le Harivel shook their hands, a gesture, Gautier supposed, to reassure them that they were not suspected of O'Flynn's murder.

'As you will understand, Messieurs,' the inspector told them, 'we are interviewing everyone who was in the hotel last night. Since I understand that you travelled down from Paris together, I assume you will have no objection to my speaking to you at the same time.'

'None whatsoever,' Gautier said. 'I hope we can be of help.'

'We certainly can, Inspector,' Duthrey said. 'You should have spoken to us sooner.'

'What can you tell me?'

'You may not have heard of the fracas at the Château Perdrix last evening. The man responsible was staying in this hotel last night.'

The interest in Le Harivel's eyes subsided. 'Are you are talking of Bishop Arkwright, Monsieur? We have already interviewed him.'

'Where is he? Under arrest?'

'When he left police headquarters a short time ago he and his companion said they intended to take a stroll in Dijon.'

'Are you saying you released him?' Duthrey was indignant.

'We had no reason to hold him. He assured us that he spent the whole of last night with the lady he is travelling with in her room.'

'And you believed him.'

'Why not? The lady in question has not denied that he did.'

In Paris Gautier left Duthrey to make his own way home from the Gare de Lyon, and found a fiacre to drive him to Sûreté headquarters on Quai des Orfèvres. He thought it unlikely that on a Sunday any crime would have been committed serious enough to require his immediate attention, but he was curious to know what would be facing him next morning.

The small pile of reports on his desk contained nothing startling. An English lady had been unwise enough, on a visit to France a few weeks previously, to invest several thousand francs in the scheme of a good-looking young man who claimed to have found gold deposits in Algeria. Now, returning to Paris, she had learnt that the young man, his luxury apartment, his château in the country and her money all appeared to have vanished. An American from Yale, a lightweight amateur boxing champion, had accepted a challenge to a fight in Pigalle, only to discover that his opponent was unsporting enough to be carrying a knife. Two middle-aged Scottish ladies had been found, helplessly drunk and carrying no form of identification, on the steps leading up to the Madeleine.

None of the incidents seemed serious. In the normal way they would scarcely have been drawn to Gautier's attention, but handled by more junior officers. What they had in common was that in all of them visitors to France were involved. Some months previously Courtrand, the Director General of the Sûreté had decided that all incidents involving British visitors should be reported to Gautier, who would see that they were fairly and courteously treated. Courtrand had a fawning respect for the British and this was to be his contribution towards preserving the fragile Entente Cordiale between France and England. After a time American visitors had been included in Gautier's special responsibility. He did not mind for it had given him an opportunity to learn more about the lives and habits of foreigners.

While he was glancing through the reports on his desk, a messenger came up to his office with an envelope which had arrived for him earlier in the day. Inside the envelope was a handwritten note.

> Jean-Paul.
> You told me that you would be returning from Dijon this afternoon. You have been promising to dine with me in my apartment for some time now. Why not tonight? Shall we say at seven-thirty? Surely you cannot refuse me again?
>
> Ingrid.

Ingrid Van de Velde was a Dutch journalist whom Gautier had met a short time previously when he was investigating the murder of a German businessman. Ingrid, who spoke German and was the Paris correspondent of a Leipzig newspaper, had been able to help him in the investigation. It was not strictly true that he had refused invitations to dine at her apartment. If anything the opposite would be nearer to the truth, for she had more than once hinted that she believed their brief friendship might grow more intimate, without once giving him an opportunity to find out whether she was being serious. Now an invitation had come and he welcomed it, for at that point there was no woman in his life. Not long previously he and Nicole, his last mistress, had agreed to end their relationship when he had learned that she had a chance to marry a colleague at the store where she worked. Since then he had spent only one night with a girl, the daughter of a wealthy banker, who had seduced him clumsily as they were travelling to Paris from Normandy. Without being vain, he supposed that Ingrid, an attractive woman who had been married to a Frenchman but was now divorced, might not be averse to starting a liaison with him. So after returning to his apartment on the Left Bank, unpacking his valise and changing, he set out on foot for the Marais, where he knew Ingrid lived. The walk was a long one, but he had plenty of time and felt he needed the exercise. For as long as he could he kept to the banks of the Seine where he felt at home. So much was always happening by the river, which seemed to have a special appeal for the people of Paris and especially on a Sunday.

The Marais itself was a historic part of Paris with fine old *hôtels particuliers* or private houses, once the homes of the aristocracy dating back to the seventeenth and eighteenth centuries. Ingrid lived in an apartment block near the Place des Vosges, which had been constructed not long ago and which, Gautier was glad to see, had been designed to a style which did not provide too much of a contrast with the ancient architecture surrounding it. Her apartment was on the third floor and as he climbed the stairs, Gautier reflected that she must be well paid as a journalist, unless of course her former husband was still providing for her. He knew little about the mechanics of divorce, which was largely the preserve of the wealthy.

She opened the door to him herself and led him to the living-room of the apartment, where she gave him an apéritif. She was a pretty, fair-haired woman with an engaging smile; the dress that she was wearing that evening showed that she had not succumbed to the fashion of the day. An elegant *maigreur* had become something of a cult among Parisiennes, to the point when, as a wit remarked, if they stood sideways-on to one they vanished. For his part Gautier still believed that a certain voluptuous amplitude was essential for true seductiveness in a woman.

'Well,' Ingrid said. 'And how was Dijon?'

'I thought it a pleasant town, not without a history of its own.'

'No doubt you meant that as praise, but it sounded so condescending.'

'Like all journalists you are always looking for hidden nuances,' Gautier grumbled.

'And did our friend Monsieur Duthrey enjoy the occasion? He told me that he was to have an honour conferred on him.'

'Yes. He was made a Chevalier of the *Confrérie du Tastevin.*'

'Was there a disturbance at the ceremony?'

'How did you know?' Gautier asked her. He found it hard to believe that news of the events in Dijon could already have reached Paris.

'I did not know, I guessed. You see I have made something of a study of Bishop Arkwright. In every place that he has visited in France he has found occasion for creating a disturbance.'

'But why does he do it? Just to promote the cause of temperance?'

Ingrid laughed. 'Not temperance, but himself. His whole tour is part of a political game.'

Bishop Arkwright's ambition, she explained, was to become the acknowledged leader of the temperance movement throughout the United States. The Anti-Saloon League, which he represented, was a powerful force in Washington, but equally powerful was the American Women's Temperance Association. The two bodies were fighting for supremacy, for what they saw as the right and the glory of leading America into Prohibition. Arkwright wished to present himself as an international figure, a world leader for the cause.

'Do you really believe that Americans will accept Prohibition?'

'It is certainly possible, eventually.'

While Ingrid was speaking, her maid came in to tell them that dinner was ready. She led them next door into the dining-room, where she served them with *foie gras*, followed by a casserole of pork with apples and prunes. Gautier wondered whether this might be a Dutch speciality. The wine they were given was a fine *premier cru* burgundy, a Mercurey, shipped by a firm named Gambon. Once again Gautier was impressed with the style of living that Ingrid enjoyed.

As they dined she continued to talk about Bishop Arkwright. 'Was there a woman with him in Dijon?' she asked Gautier.

'There was. I do not know her name, but she was in her forties, I suppose, attractive, and elegantly dressed but without ostentation.'

'Is not *soignée* the word a Frenchwoman would use to describe her?'

'Exactly. I concluded that she was not his wife.'

Ingrid smiled. 'Trust a Frenchman to notice. How did you deduce that?'

'They were both staying in the same hotel as I was, but had reserved separate rooms.'

'That would be Mrs Barclay, a wealthy widow. The bishop has a wife, but she is in America.'

'You seem remarkably well informed about Bishop Arkwright.'

'As I told you, I am following his visit to France closely.'

'May I ask why?'

'Because I believe that in due course his escapades may provide material for a story in the American papers.'

'But you work for a German newspaper, do you not?'

'Principally, and I write a political column for *Le Gaulois*. As you know I am a linguist, so papers in other countries do from time to time print what I write. In due course, what I would like is to be officially connected with an American daily.'

'Have you any particular paper in mind?'

'The *Washington Post*. It is in Washington that all the political battles are waged, including the campaign for Prohibition. If I can get some good stories about Bishop Arkwright accepted by the *Post*, it may be the first step towards my becoming its Paris correspondent.'

Gautier was trying to decide whether he should tell Ingrid more about what had happened in Dijon. In the normal way he never discussed police matters with his friends, but in this case the murder of Michael O'Flynn was not in his jurisdiction and he remembered that Ingrid had been of help to him in his last major investigation. He could see no harm in mentioning that Arkwright had apparently spent the night in Mrs Barclay's bedroom.

'That does not surprise me,' Ingrid said. 'The bishop has been involved in more than his share of scandals. Once he was proved to have fraudulently used his church's money to play the stock-market and on another occasion he was caught *in flagrante delicto* with another woman in a New York hotel. The Methodist Church took no action. He seems able to get away with murder.'

Gautier tried not to show his amusement at the aptness of her last remark in the circumstances of Arkwright's predicament in Dijon. Even so Ingrid must have noticed a change in his expression, for she at once accused him:

'You have not told me everything you know, have you?'

'No, not everything.'

'Why not?'

He knew then that he would have to tell her about the murder of Michael O'Flynn. She would know soon enough for in due course it would be reported, even though briefly, in the Paris newspapers. As he described what had happened, he could sense that her brain was busy, working out how she could use the information to her professional advantage.

He finished by saying, 'If you mention the murder in your story, I hope you will not insinuate that the bishop might have been responsible.'

'Of course not! You are not suggesting that any journalist would print innuendoes simply to sell newspapers?'

'It has been known.'

'Don't be cynical,' Ingrid reproved him as she refilled both their glasses with wine.

She evidently had no more questions to ask about Bishop Arkwright and they began to talk of other things; of Paris, the theatre, the paintings that had been exhibited at that year's Salon, the declining influence of art nouveau after a decade of dominance in graphic design and interior decoration. Presently her mood seemed to change and she began to tease him. That was a good sign, he told himself, for as a general rule people only teased those for whom they felt an affection.

They continued talking after they had left the table and returned to the drawing-room. Although they were sitting side by side on a sofa, she gave no sign that she was expecting any of the advances that most French men would certainly have made in such circumstances. Attractive women did not invite men to dine tête-à-tête with them in their apartments merely for conversation, however cultured. The Dutch, he had always understood, were more reserved than the French and it was possible that she might be waiting for him to make the first demonstration of his feelings. He had never been one to force his attentions on a woman, but the wine they had drunk was loosening his inhibitions. So he decided he might remind her of the half-promise she had made to him on an earlier occasion.

'Is this evening to be the start of the new intimacy which you forecast for us?' he asked her.

'I hope it is, although not in the way that you may have been expecting.' She looked at him, smiling. 'Be patient, Jean-Paul. There will be other evenings, other nights, I promise you, but tonight I have work to do.'

'Work?'

'A story to write. I must telegraph a piece on Bishop Arkwright's misadventures to the *Washington Post*. Taking into account the difference in time, it might just reach the news desk before they go to press with tomorrow morning's edition.'

'If that is the case, perhaps I should leave you now so you can make a start on the story.'

'Oh, I will not write it here, but at my office. Then I can telegraph it immediately to America.'

They left her apartment together and found a fiacre at the corner of the street. Even though she protested that she would be taking him well out of his way home, Gautier insisted on dropping her off outside her offices in Rue Réaumur. In the darkness she took his arm and snuggled up to him.

'Are you very disappointed, *chéri*?' she asked him softly.

'I would be lying if I said I was not, but I understand.'

Leaning across, she kissed him on the cheek and then, turning his face towards her, on the mouth. For a moment they were united by a surge of passion and then she pulled away. Gautier supposed that the kiss was intended as another promise, a promise for the future. He could not help hoping that she would not spoil it by telling him that one day she would make up to him for the evening's disappointment.

What she did say was, 'You will be thinking that I have just been using you.'

'Nonsense!'

After she had left him and as he was being driven across Paris towards the Left Bank, Gautier recognized that Ingrid had invited him to dine with her for a purpose. She had learned somehow that Bishop Arkwright was to be in Dijon and had reasoned that if he had caused any trouble, Gautier would have heard of it. He had told her what she had hoped to hear and now she was writing the story for Washington. Of course she had been using him, but rather to his surprise, he found that he did not really mind.

3

Next morning at Sûreté headquarters Gautier began to deal with the reports which he had found waiting for him when he returned from Dijon. Most of what he had to do was not so much police work as diplomacy. He dealt first with the matter of the two Scottish ladies, not because it was the most urgent, but because he was approached early in the day with a plea for action. He had not been long in his office when he was told that an official from the British embassy in Paris had arrived at Quai des Orfèvres asking to see him. It was not a request that he could reasonably refuse.

The official, a third secretary named Benson, appeared embarrassed by the favour that he was going to ask of Gautier. The embassy had been shocked to learn early that morning that the two ladies had spent a night in a police cell. They were ladies of unimpeachable virtue, Benson claimed, both from the Highlands of Scotland and socially well connected. Their behaviour on the steps of the Madeleine, which they had mistakenly believed to be the residence of the President of France, had been the result of an unfortunate misunderstanding. In Scotland it was not unknown for even respectable women of mature years to drink whisky. Indeed in a country where everyone had to be fortified against the rigours of the climate, one might say it was the accepted daily drink for everyone, men and women alike. For women though it was almost always diluted with lemonade. Here it was that the two ladies had been unwittingly led astray. After dining well and perhaps too well in their hotel, they had decided to go out and sample the atmosphere of the real Paris in a café on Boulevard des Capucines. There they ordered two Scotch whiskies with lemonade. Whisky had only recently made an appearance in France, but could be obtained in a few of the better known cafés. Lemonade was a different matter. No one had ever heard of this strange Scottish drink. The two ladies had insisted that their whiskies should be diluted and eventually, after a discussion largely unintelligible because of linguistic difficulties, the waiter had produced what he decided was a near equivalent of lemonade. It was in fact a liqueur made from wormwood, which had an alcohol content well above that of any drink known in Scotland and the waiter had added it generously to the whiskies. The Scottish ladies had so enjoyed this powerful cocktail, that they had ordered two more. After three drinks each, they had decided that they must call on the President of France to thank him personally for the way they had been treated by the friendly Parisians.

'I understand that they got as far as the Madeleine,' Benson told Gautier, 'where their eccentric behaviour attracted the attention of two gendarmes and they were taken into custody, more for their own protection than any breach of the law.'

'Have you seen them this morning?' Gautier asked.

'Not as yet, but I am told that both ladies are full of remorse and ashamed of what happened. If news should reach Edinburgh that they had appeared in the courts, they would be disgraced.' Benson paused before he added, 'The embassy would be very grateful if that could in some way be avoided.'

Gautier smiled. 'I am sure that can be arranged, Monsieur.

Perhaps if someone could be found to give a surety for their future good behaviour?'

'Of course. Sir Donald would be delighted to do that, delighted!' Sir Donald Macnab, Gautier knew, was the British Ambassador in Paris.

'In that case I will arrange for them to be released immediately into your custody.'

After repeated protestations of his gratitude, Benson left to collect the two ladies and no doubt to put them on the first boat train for London. His success even in such a trifling mission would be noted in high quarters and in due course would help in his career. Gautier found himself wondering whether by any chance the two ladies might be distantly related to the ambassador himself.

Not long after Benson had left two more visitors arrived. Charles Dwight, the boxer from Yale, came accompanied by a French lawyer whom he had retained to advise him. Dwight spoke no French and although Gautier's rudimentary English had improved in recent months, he felt it was better to carry on their discussions through the lawyer.

'Have you arrested the scoundrel who attacked my client?' the lawyer asked.

'Not as yet, Monsieur, but it is only a question of time.' Gautier's answer was truthful. The fight had taken place in a seedy café in Pigalle where onlookers would know the name of the *voyou* who had knifed Dwight. No one had come forward yet to name the attacker, but it was only a matter of time. A rival, a jealous pimp, a disgruntled prostitute, would in due course whisper a name to the police.

'I am sure you are right, Inspector, but this places Monsieur Dwight in some difficulty. He is due to sail for New York from Cherbourg on Wednesday and would not wish to delay his return simply to give evidence in court proceedings.'

'I must return home to continue my studies,' Dwight said. 'I cannot afford to miss graduation.'

'I understand, Monsieur.'

Dwight was carrying his right arm in a sling, but beyond that he did not appear to be seriously wounded. Gautier supposed that when he had faced up to his assailant in the café, he had adopted the boxer's classic stance, but before he could lead with his left in the way of all boxers, he had been given a quick knife slash in the fleshy part of his right arm. In all probability it was only his pride that was really hurt.

'When we discover who attacked your client, he will of course be charged,' Gautier told the lawyer, 'but I do not think it will be necessary for Monsieur Dwight to be present at the hearing. In the meantime the Sûreté will issue a statement calling for witnesses, perhaps even offering a reward. The statement will also make a point of thanking Monsieur Dwight for tackling an armed criminal and congratulating him on his gallantry.'

'Would it be possible for me to be given a copy of the statement?' Dwight asked.

'I will have one sent to your hotel this afternoon, Monsieur.'

As the American and his lawyer were leaving, Gautier decided that for a Monday the morning had begun well. Very often Mondays could be awkward, not because the problems left over from the weekend were difficult, but because very often the people who came to see him had spent Sunday brooding over whatever predicament their foolishness had placed them in and arrived determined either to defend themselves truculently or to be obstructive, saying nothing. That morning he had dealt easily and, what was more important, rapidly, with the indiscretions of two Scottish ladies and the injured vanity of a young American. He looked at the next report, wondering how best to tackle the problem of the English lady who had parted with her money too read-ily. Before he had reached any conclusion he was interrupted by a message saying that the Director General wished to see him.

Gustave Courtrand was not a professional policeman. His appointment as Director General of the Sûreté had been a piece of political patronage, a return by some government minister for favours done in the past. As a figurehead he was useful, making the right noises on public occasions, but when from time to time he tried to involve himself in the administration of the Sûreté, the results were always irritating, sometimes disastrous. When Gautier arrived in his office he began talking about his latest *bête noire*, the Métro. The building of Paris's underground railway had been begun some ten years previously; some lines had already been constructed and were in use. Courtrand distrusted the Métro as he did all mechanical contrivances. He would not even use the telephone which had recently been installed in the offices of senior officials in the Sûreté, but made his secretary answer it for him.

'Were you aware that some of our policemen have begun to use the Métro?' he asked Gautier.

'No, Monsieur.'

'When they leave headquarters on an assignment, they should walk. It is reassuring for the people of Paris to see police officers in the street, to know that they have our protection.'

'The Métro could be useful in emergencies, as a means of saving time. One can travel across Paris by it so swiftly.'

'I would like you as a matter of priority to draw up a code of regulations governing the use of the Métro by all grades of staff.'

Gautier realized that Courtrand was not even listening to what he had to say. It was one of the more irritating of his many irritating habits. One could only listen and make polite noises from time to time. He listened while Courtrand was thinking aloud, improvizing rules which might be included in the code.

Eventually he came to the matter which was the whole point behind his idea.

'You must make it clear,' he said, 'that any officer, whatever his rank, if he should be obliged to use the Métro must travel second class.'

The fares on the Métro were standard whatever the journey. The first-class fare was twenty-five centimes and the second-class fifteen centimes. Courtrand's purpose in suggesting the rule was not economy, to cut a few centimes from the Sûreté's budget, but to distance the lower ranks from himself in the matter of travel. He had a carriage and a coachman at his disposal for any journeys he might need to make and he could now be afraid of losing this privilege, of being obliged to travel on the Métro, where he might meet other officers of junior rank. That was the way the man's mind worked.

Gautier's meeting with Courtrand that morning – one could scarcely call it a conversation – had been comparatively and mercifully brief. As he returned to his office he was thinking that he might have enough time before lunch to deal with the complaint of the English lady victim of a confidence trickster. The report on his desk had given the name of the hotel in which she was staying. His optimism was premature for when he reached office he found Surat, his principal assistant, waiting outside his door. One of Surat's duties was to deal with visitors who arrived at Sûreté headquarters asking to see Gautier. In the past year or two Parisians had become increasingly aware of Gautier's achievements in solving criminal cases and a good number would come hoping that he might be able to help them with some small problem that faced them. Surat would act as a kind of screen, turning most of them away or giving them what help or advice he could.

'There is a Monsieur Philippe Gambon downstairs,' he told Gautier.

'What does he want?'

'That is not entirely clear, but he claims to be from Dijon.' Surat knew that Gautier had been in Dijon over the weekend and by now he might even have heard of the murder that had been committed there, though that seemed unlikely. 'I thought you might be interested to hear what he has to say.'

'In that case bring him up to my office.'

Philippe Gambon must have been in his mid-thirties; he was tall and good looking. Everything about him, his clothes, his neatly trimmed moustaches and beard helped to reinforce that air of self-assurance which comes from a good education, wealth, or both. He handed Gautier a business card on which were printed his name and that of the firm he represented.

LUCIEN GAMBON ET FILS

Négociants-en-vins, Dijon, Beaune et Paris

Philippe Gambon *Directeur Commercial*

As he read the card, Gautier remembered where he had seen the name Gambon before. It had been on the label of the bottle of wine which Ingrid had served him at dinner the previous evening. That he supposed could only be a coincidence. He was not a connoisseur of wine, but as far as he knew the firm of Gambon was not among the major wine-shippers of France. He showed the young man to a chair and they sat facing each other across his desk.

'How can I be of assistance to you, Monsieur?'

'You were in Dijon on Saturday, at the banquet of the *Confrérie du Tastevin*, were you not?'

'I was. By invitation. Were you there?'

Gambon smiled. 'Unfortunately not. I am from Dijon, but now I live in exile in Paris. I run the branch of our family business here. In fact I spent the whole of last weekend in Bordeaux, where we are hoping to make business arrangements with some of the wine-producers in the region. Friends from home told me that you were to be one of the guests at the banquet.'

Gautier made no comment so Gambon went on, 'Did you by any chance meet a Monsieur Armand Pascal in Dijon?'

'As it happens I did. He sat next to me at the banquet. Why?'

'I am surprised he was there. He is no friend of Michael O'Flynn.'

Gautier waited. He had the feeling that Gambon had more to say about the relationship between Pascal and O'Flynn.

After a long pause Gambon went on, 'O'Flynn was determined to buy Pascal's vineyard.'

'And Pascal had no wish to sell?'

'No, but he is in a difficult position. He is heavily in debt. He is being squeezed out of the wine business.'

'Are you suggesting, Monsieur, that this enmity may be in some way connected with the murder of Michael O'Flynn?'

'Then you heard about the murder?'

'Monsieur O'Flynn was killed in the hotel where I was staying.'

'Le Chapeau Rouge? I had no idea.' Gambon paused, then he said apologetically, 'Inspector, I certainly was not accusing Pascal. He could never be involved in a murder. You met him so you will know he is not that type of man.' Again Gautier waited, curious to learn in what direction Gambon would steer their conversation. 'So you are investigating this murder?'

'Not me, Monsieur. It is the responsibility of the police in Dijon.'

'They should have no difficulty in solving it. Dijon is a small place. It cannot house many murderers.'

'I am glad you are so confident.'

'It's true. Dijon is small and the wine trade is a tiny community, almost incestuous, one might say, as of all small communities. You would be surprised how small. I know everyone of any importance in it. Many of them are related to my family, at least distantly. Why, only a few months ago, a nephew of Michael O'Flynn's wife, or should I say widow, married one of my brother's cousins.'

'You have a brother, Monsieur?'

'Oh yes; an elder brother. He runs our vineyard back home.'

'Then your family owns a vineyard?' Gautier had always been under the impression that *négociants* did not own vineyards, but bought the *vendanges* or the wines of others which they bottled, sometimes blended, and sold.

'A very small one; not much more than two hectares. My father bought it a year or two ago, only I suspect to give my brother something to occupy himself with, while I run the firm's Paris office.'

They talked for a little longer, Gambon telling Gautier more about developments in the wine business. Bordeaux wines, clarets as the English called them, were already being shipped to countries outside France and demand for them seemed certain to expand, particularly in America as more and more wealthy Americans travelled to Europe and learnt about French life and culture. Gautier did not mind listening to him, as it was always useful to learn about the *métiers* of other people. At the same time he was curious about why Gambon had come to see him that morning. He may well have believed that Gautier would be in charge of investigating the murder of Michael O'Flynn, for most Frenchmen had only the vaguest idea of how the police services of the country operated. Even if that were so, he appeared to have almost no information about the murder that might have been helpful to the authorities. One was tempted to think that he had come, not to give information, but to find out how much Gautier knew. That at once prompted questions about his motives.

When Gambon finally left, Gautier tried to contact the English lady who had been swindled of her money. Her name was Lady Jane Shelford and Surat had ascertained that she was staying at the Hôtel Cheltenham. He telephoned the hotel and was told that Lady Jane was out and was not expected to return for lunch. She would have gone out shopping, Gautier supposed, and would be lunching at one of Paris's many fine restaurants. French ladies of good standing never lunched away from their homes. Indeed they would seldom go out during the day, except perhaps to take a drive in the Bois de Boulogne or a stroll in Rue des Acacias, saving their energies for the distractions of the evening, for a visit to l'Opéra or the Comédie Française or the circus, followed by dinner with friends at Le Grand Véfour or Le Doyen. English ladies did not know, or would not conform to, the conventions of French society and often behaved with an independent freedom.

When he realized that he would not be able to speak to Lady Jane that morning, Gautier decided he would go to the Café Corneille in Boulevard St Germain. He would find the time most days to take an apéritif at the café with his friends. Cafés were a fundamental part of social life in Paris for men who did not aspire to membership of the Jockey Club, the Cercle du Rue Royale or any of the other exclusive clubs, modelled on the English pattern. One could find cafés in Paris which catered for every profession or *métier*; cafés for stockbrokers, jewellers, circus-performers. The Café Corneille had a wider selection of habitués, drawn from the law, politics and an occasional academic from the university nearby.

That morning Gautier found Duthrey there, surrounded by a small circle of other friends and he guessed that they would be talking about the *Confrérie des Chevaliers du Tastevin*. They were, and Duthrey was passing round the silver *tastevin* which had been presented to him at Dijon. The others were full of admiration.

'This is a singular honour that has been accorded to you, my friend,' an elderly judge was saying. 'One supposes that you must be the only person outside the wine business to have received it.'

'So far, yes.'

Everyone in the circle repeated their congratulations, solemnly shaking Duthrey's hand. Gautier had always found the passion of the French for decorations slightly comical, but he hid his amusement as Froissart, who ran a bookshop on the Left Bank and knew something about silverware, praised the workmanship of the *tastevin*. He had no intention of spoiling Duthrey's enjoyment by telling their friends of how the induction ceremony had been interrupted by Bishop Arkwright, but to his surprise Duthrey did.

'Can you believe it?' Duthrey asked them after he had described the incident, 'that lunatic has come here, crossing the Atlantic, in the belief that he can persuade us French to abandon drinking.'

Everyone laughed. Most well-informed Frenchmen would have read about the temperance movement which had swept America and, to a lesser extent, England over the past hundred years, but few had ever even considered that it might take root in Europe. Only one of those at the Café Comeille that morning, the deputy for Seine-et-Marne, had any first-hand knowledge of how the apostles of the movement were operating in Europe.

'In addition to this bishop,' he told the others, 'an American woman is here in Paris who claims that she represents the American Women's Temperance Association and that she speaks for millions of women in America. She and Bishop Arkwright are bitter rivals and are said to detest each other. Do you know she has had the effrontery to suggest that she should be allowed to address a joint meeting of both chambers of our parliament?'

'She is not being allowed to, is she?' Froissart asked.

'Over my dead body!' the deputy said indignantly. 'The department which I have the honour to represent produces champagne, a drink for which France is justly famous and which is drunk throughout the world. If I were even to listen to this American woman, my people would rise in arms. Temperance indeed!'

'What is her name?' Gautier asked. He had the feeling that if the woman's style of proselytizing was as aggressive as Bishop Arkwright's, she might well fall foul of the police while she was in Paris.

'Mademoiselle Stephanie Winstock. All her women friends know her as Steve. She is touring Europe with a soi-disant secretary named Pauline Fenn.'

'Our noble French wines are only now recovering from the disaster of phylloxera,' the judge said. 'The last thing our vine-growers want is interference by American busybodies.'

He was referring to the phylloxera insect, a species of greenfly, which had ravaged the vineyards of France in the years following 1860. It had taken many experiments and much patient determination to eliminate the disease which phylloxera had caused and only in the last two decades had the great wines of France been restored to their former excellence.

'I have always understood,' Gautier said, 'that phylloxera came to this country from America.'

'That is true,' Duthrey told him, 'and ironically in the end the only way our vines could be saved was by grafting them on to American stock, which by that time was immune to the disease.'

'I think we can be sure,' the deputy said pompously, 'that having survived a natural disaster from America, we French will not allow ourselves to be duped into accepting a man-made one manufactured by religious zealots.'

'You call phylloxera a disaster,' Duthrey said, 'but many perceptive lovers of wine believe it may have been a blessing in disguise.'

'A blessing! I understood it has cost the equivalent of almost two thousand million francs in gold to rectify!'

Duthrey explained that only after the ravages of phylloxera had the wine-growers begun to tackle the problems which had always faced the wine industry; problems caused by the planting of inferior strains of grape, by over-production, by poor techniques of vinification. Now the problems had been tackled and new standards were being laid down which would end in a properly controlled system of definitions and appellations. Listening to him explaining all this, Gautier could understand why Duthrey had been invited to be a member of the *Confrérie des Chevaliers du Tastevin*. Duthrey had given him a copy of the book he had written and he was ashamed that so far he had not even started to read it.

Later when he and Duthrey had left the café and were walking down Boulevard St Germain looking for a fiacre, Duthrey returned to the subject of temperance. He remarked, 'You may well see more of Bishop Arkwright before too long.'

'What makes you think that?'

'He and his lady companion are in Paris. In fact they must have left Dijon at much the same time as we did, possibly travelling by the same train.'

'How do you know this?'

'*Figaro* is keeping a check on his movements. Most of the newspapers in Paris are.' Duthrey clearly did not enjoy talking about the bishop. The memory of his behaviour at the banquet still upset him. 'He came to Europe simply to get publicity for himself and he is succeeding.'

'Do you know where he and Mrs Barclay are staying?'

'At the Hôtel Cheltenham.'

As he was crossing the Seine by the Pont Neuf, Gautier told himself it could only be a coincidence that Bishop Arkwright should be staying at the same hotel as Lady Jane Shelford. When he left Dijon he had assumed that he would hear no more of the murder of Michael O'Flynn. Then Philippe Gambon had arrived to remind him about it. Now if he were to visit the Hôtel Cheltenham to speak to Lady Jane there was at least a possibility that he might see the bishop.

When he arrived at Sûreté headquarters he found Surat waiting for him with a message.

'The police from Dijon telephoned,' he told Gautier. 'An inspector.'

'Inspector Le Harivel?'

'That is correct. He will be in Paris tomorrow and has asked if he can come and see you on a matter of some importance.'

4

Inspector Le Harivel came to see Gautier at Sûreté headquarters soon after noon next day, having travelled up by train from Dijon. He was not wearing uniform and for this reason seemed somehow smaller and less imposing. After the usual exchange of courtesies, he came directly to the reason for his visit.

'I understand, Monsieur Gautier, that at the banquet of the *Confrérie des Chevaliers du Tastevin* you were sitting next to a Monsieur Armand Pascal.' When Gautier admitted that that was so, Le Harivel continued, 'I have also been told that on the morning after the murder of Monsieur O'Flynn you spent some time talking to Pascal in the lobby of the hotel.'

'That is true. I did.'

'May I know what you were talking about?'

'He was questioning me about the murder. He thought that I might be in charge of the investigation. I could tell him nothing, of course.'

'Did he say what he was doing in Dijon? As you may know he does not live in the city.'

'Apparently he was there to meet two business associates who were arriving that morning by train from Paris.'

'He does not seem to have been seen that morning talking to visitors either at the railway station or elsewhere.'

Le Harivel was silent for a time. The questions he had so far asked were trivial enough and Gautier could not help wondering why the man had come to see him. Paris had many attractions for those who lived in the provinces and it was not unknown for country policemen to find an excuse for visiting the capital and sampling some of its pleasures. On the other hand perhaps he did have a matter which he wished to discuss with Gautier, but had not decided how to raise it.

Eventually Le Harivel said, 'It has been suggested to us that Pascal may have had a grudge against Michael O'Flynn.'

'Because O'Flynn was trying to buy his vineyard?'

'So you have heard that too?'

'Yes, but not from a source which I would necessarily believe to be reliable.'

Le Harivel did not ask who the source was, but Gautier's comment seemed in some way to put him at ease, to relax whatever inhibitions had been making him reluctant to talk. He said, 'We would like to ask Pascal some questions about that, but he seems to have disappeared.'

'Disappeared?'

'He is not at his home. His wife and two children have not seen him since he left to go to the banquet on Saturday evening.'

'So you do not know where he spent that night?'

'No, nor Sunday night. Friends of his have suggested that he may have come to Paris.'

Now Gautier could understand why Le Harivel had come to see him; he could also understand his anxiety. If Pascal had in any way been connected with the murder of O'Flynn, he should at least be questioned. Rumours would be spreading; the local police would be under pressure to provide an explanation for his disappearance. If he had in fact come to Paris it would be difficult for them to find him.

Gautier took out his pocket-watch. It would soon be one o'clock; too late for him to go to the Café Corneille and almost time for lunch.

'My friend,' he said, 'why do not you and I go and discuss this matter over lunch?'

They lunched at a modest café in Place Dauphine, only a couple of minutes' walk from Sûreté headquarters, where Gautier often ate. The café had once been owned by a woman from Normandy, and her daughter Janine who for a time had been Gautier's mistress, but they had sold the place and returned to Normandy where, he had heard, Janine had married a farmer. He remembered her with nostalgia and although the standard of the cuisine had, if anything, declined since her time he still used the place.

That day as there was no major trial being conducted at the Palais de Justice nearby, the café was not crowded and he and Le Harivel were given a table where they could talk freely. After they had spent several minutes on the more serious business of studying the menu and deciding what they would eat, Gautier felt he might raise the matter of O'Flynn's murder.

'Is it true that when the dead man was found he was wearing a cardinal's hat?' he asked Le Harivel.

'Yes, but I suspect that may only have been the murderer's way of confusing us, of throwing suspicion on the American bishop, who was staying at the hotel that night.'

'I can see that, but where would the murderer have found a cardinal's hat at that time of night? Surely he could not have brought it with him?'

'No. The hat had evidently been taken from a glass case in the dining-room, where there was a small display illustrating the history of the hotel.'

'If your theory is right the murderer must have been at the *intronisation* ceremony that evening.'

'It seems so, or at least that he had heard of the contretemps that took place there.'

As they lunched Le Harivel spoke of the enquiries that the Dijon police had so far made into the murder of O'Flynn. They had established that O'Flynn had intended to spend the night after the banquet in Dijon and had reserved a room at the Hostellerie du Chapeau Rouge. The reason for this was not clear but one might suppose he did not wish to make the journey so late at night to the Château Perdrix, where he and his family lived. When the banquet and the ceremony were over, he and the other officers of the *Confrérie* had driven to Dijon. where they had held a meeting to review the events of the evening and to assess the success of the *intronisation*. After the meeting with the other officers ended, O'Flynn had been given a key to his room on the first floor by the concierge and had gone straight upstairs.

'But he never went into the room, did he?' Gautier asked.

'We believe he did; that he was stabbed to death in his room some time later and his body was then dragged into the corridor, where it was found early in the morning by one of the maids when she came on duty.'

'Then O'Flynn must have admitted the murderer into his room?'

'It would appear so.'

Le Harivel continued eating in silence for a time. Then he added, 'I am beginning to wonder whether we may not have been premature in eliminating the bishop as a possible suspect of the murder. We only have his companion Madame Barclay's word that he spent the whole night in her room.'

'If you were thinking of questioning him again, I can tell you where you can find him. He and Mrs Barclay are staying at the Hôtel Cheltenham.

Le Harivel glanced quickly across at Gautier. One could sense suspicion as well as surprise in his look and he must have been wondering whether the Sûreté had started its own investigation into the murder of O'Flynn.

To reassure him Gautier added, 'By a coincidence an Englishwoman, who is involved in another, totally separate matter which we are investigating, is staying at the same hotel.'

'Are you planning to speak to him?'

'Not unless you ask me to officially.'

'What I would like the Sûreté to do is to help us find Pascal.'

'Willingly. When he have finished lunch we can go back to my office and decide how that can best be done.'

Lady Jane was on Gautier's conscience. He had managed to settle the problems of two Scottish ladies and an American college student, but the Englishwoman's complaint was still on file. So after Le Harivel had left to catch his train, he telephoned the Hôtel Cheltenham and was told that Lady Jane Shelford was in her suite and would be willing to see him.

In her looks and manner Lady Jane was very much what Gautier had expected she might be; a typical Englishwoman almost ready to surrender to approaching middle age. He had often told himself that one should not judge a person, and particularly a woman, by her appearance and her clothes, but now he found himself doing just that. She received him in the drawing-room of her suite and in Gautier's opinion the outfit she was wearing did nothing for her; a long grey coat, severe in cut and a matching toque hat of the style which had gone out of fashion some years previously. Her gloves, which she had taken off, were lying in her lap and were surprisingly wrinkled and worn.

'Well, Inspector, have you found the scoundrel who robbed me?' Her French was fluent enough, but, like everything else about her, stiff and precise.

'I regret not, Madame, but as yet you have told us so little about the gentleman.'

'Gentleman!' She snorted. 'But then I suppose he must have been a gentleman or I would never have been introduced to him.'

'Where did you meet him?'

'At a soirée given by the Comtesse de Fleury. That was our first meeting. I was in Paris for a month at the time and we met again later. He took me driving in the Bois de Boulogne.'

'Alone?'

'Certainly not!' Lady Jane's indignation seemed genuine enough. 'Miss Boyle, my travelling companion, chaperoned us.'

Miss Boyle had been in the suite that afternoon when Gautier arrived, but had been sent to her own room in another part of the hotel. Obviously chaperons were not considered essential when a lady was being interviewed by a policeman. Gautier remembered that it had been in the Hôtel Cheltenham a few years back that a lady's companion had been accused of murdering her employer, also an English milady. She had been in prison for a time until he was able to prove her innocence.

'What was the name of this gentleman, may I ask?'

'Desfontaines. Pierre Desfontaines. Look, I have his card.' She handed him a card which was similar in style to the cards handed out by most business men in Paris.

PIERRE DESFONTAINES

Ingénieur Conseil

Membre de l'Académie des Sciences.

Gautier had never heard of the Académie des Sciences, nor of the address printed on the card. Both could well be bogus, but the card, supported by the fact that her ladyship had met Desfontaines in the home of the Comtesse de Fleury, had evidently been enough to dispel any suspicions Lady Jane might have had about him.

She was not reluctant to talk. Slowly, by patiently structuring his questions, Gautier learned the story. After their first meeting, her acquaintance with Desfontaines had developed rapidly. He had invited her to join him at the races at Longchamps, escorted her to a *vernissage*, or private viewing of an exhibition of paintings at a fashionable gallery, taken her to dine at Fouquet's. Almost casually Desfontaines had told her of his family's social connections and of their fine old château in the country. Equally casually he had mentioned his business interests and how he and an associate had discovered gold in Algeria, which only a shortage of capital was preventing them from exploiting. Lady Jane had agreed to help. She would not tell Gautier the size of the loan she had given to Desfontaines but it had run into six figures. It had been a classic confidence trick, skilfully and elegantly handled.

'Then unexpectedly I had to come to Paris again. When I knew I was coming,' Lady Jane said, 'I wrote to Monsieur Desfontaines but had no reply.'

'Did you try to contact him in any other way?'

'I asked the Comtesse de Fleury if she could tell me how I might reach him, but she said she had never heard of any Monsieur Desfontaines. I suppose that is possible. He might have been taken to the reception by another guest. There were so many people there that evening.'

'We will make our own enquiries,' Gautier told her. 'If he has done this kind of thing before, there is every chance that he can be traced.'

'And if you succeed, would I get my money back?'

'That depends; did you enter into any formal arrangement? Was there anything in writing?'

'No. In England we assume that one can rely on the word of a gentleman.'

'Then was anyone else present when Desfontaines persuaded you to invest money in his project? Your travelling companion?'

Lady Jane did not look at Gautier as she shook her head. He had the impression that she was almost blushing at having to admit that she had spoken to a gentleman unaccompanied by her chaperon. Perhaps this English milady was not as aloof and austere as her manner suggested. Even so he was beginning to believe there was very little chance that she would ever get her money back.

'You are not a regular visitor to Paris then?' Gautier asked her.

'No. I came once or twice with my parents when I was younger, but until my last visit I had not been here for years. To be frank, I am not very fond of the French. On the rare occasions that I travel, I prefer to go to Germany. I find it much more civilized.'

'Did Desfontaines know this?'

'I may have mentioned it.'

There were other questions that he should ask her, but before he could they heard a knock on the door of the room which led to the corridor outside. Lady Jane answered. One of the hotel's pageboys opened the door and ushered in a short, red-haired woman. When Lady Jane saw who the woman was, she jumped up and gave a little cry of delight.

'Steve!' The two women embraced warmly, and for a little longer than mere friendship might have demanded. Then Lady Jane stepped back and they looked at each other, smiling.

'Steve darling, you have not changed at all!'

'Nor have you, darling.'

Gautier realized that this could only be the Stephanie Winstock about whom the deputy for Seine-et-Marne had spoken at the Café Corneille that morning. He watched her as she and Lady Jane exchanged endearments in English. Besides being auburn, Miss Winstock's hair was cut short, which accentuated the severe contours of her face. No one could have thought her beautiful, but behind the severity of her expression and the pince-nez she was wearing, Gautier sensed a charm which she could deploy when, as now, it suited her. He supposed that she would be much the same age as Lady Jane, but she looked older.

'I have bad news for you darling,' Lady Jane seemed suddenly to remember something she had to tell Miss Winstock. 'Your enemy, Bishop Arkwright, is staying in this hotel.'

'I don't believe it!' Miss Winstock looked shocked, but then she laughed. 'So much the better! You will be able to spy on him and let me know what imbecilities he is planning.'

'And some woman is with him; I have a good mind to complain to the management.'

'Don't bother, darling. I can handle the old rogue.'

Lady Jane looked at Gautier. She had not introduced him to her visitor and seemed to have forgotten he was there. Now that she remembered, she decided she could dispense with him.

'Inspector, have we finished our discussion? Miss Winstock and I have not met for almost a year, so we have so much catching up to do.'

Gautier accepted the dismissal. 'Of course, Lady Jane. We will be in touch again in due course no doubt.'

As he left the room he heard Lady Jane saying. 'How did you find me, darling? Wasn't it clever of you?'

When he returned to his office from the Hôtel Cheltenham Gautier found a letter waiting for him, which had been delivered at the Sûreté by hand. He saw that it was from Ingrid Van de Velde, no more than a note written by hand and attached to a typewritten article. The note was brief:

> Chéri, this is piece which I telegraphed to the Washington Post. Whether they will use all or any of it remains to be seen. Wish me luck with it! I look forward to hearing your opinion. I shall be in my apartment early this evening.
>
> Yours, Ingrid.

The article was in English and was headed:

AMERICAN BISHOP IN FRENCH MURDER ENQUIRY

James Arkwright, a Methodist bishop from Ohio was one of those questioned by police in Dijon, France in connection with the murder of a leading French vineyard owner on Sunday night. The bishop had earlier gatecrashed a banquet of the prestigious *Confrérie des Chevaliers du Tastevin* held in a medieval hall at a wine château, where he is alleged to have created a disturbance and to have been forcibly evicted. The bishop is one of the leading figures in America's Anti-Saloon League and the purpose of his visit to France is to spread the message of temperance to Europe. He has already caused disturbances in French restaurants, cafés and on several public occasions where alcohol was being served. Earlier this month he was asked to leave a wine auction in Bordeaux, when he attempted to interrupt the proceedings with a diatribe against wine and so to prevent any business being done. The bishop's travels in Europe are not being financed by the Anti-Saloon League, nor by his church, but by Mrs Deborah Barclay, a wealthy New York widow who is accompanying him on his tour.

As he read the article Gautier began to wonder whether Ingrid realized that Arkwright was now in Paris. Arkwright and Stephanie Winstock were known to be rivals and the deputy for Seine-et-Marne had said that they disliked each other intensely. If on one of Stephanie's visits to see her friend Lady Jane, they ran into each other, given the bishop's belligerent rudeness one could see that trouble might well arise. If that were to happen, Gautier would prefer to be ready and to intervene before it escalated. He was on very good terms with the management of the Hôtel Cheltenham and if possible he would like to spare the hotel the embarrassment of a public scandal.

He read Ingrid's note again. In it she had told him that she would be at home early that evening and it was not unreasonable to assume that this was an invitation for him to call and see her. She might of course merely wish to hear his opinion on her article, but could she have another motive as well? The frustration he had felt two nights ago when their tête-à-tête dinner had been brought to an early conclusion still lingered.

So, after sending for Surat and putting in train one or two further measures to find out whether Pascal was in Paris and where he was staying, he left the Sûreté, and headed for the Marais. It was just after six when he reached Ingrid's apartment, a little earlier perhaps than she had intended, but it should leave time for the evening to develop in a number of rewarding ways.

When she opened the door to him she appeared delighted and kissed him affectionately. 'So you could come! That's wonderful! What do you think of my article?'

'Are we going to discuss it here on the doorstep?'

'Of course not! Come on in and we'll take a glass of wine as we talk.'

A bottle of wine and two glasses were standing on a table in the living-room. So, Gautier thought, she had been confident that he would come to see her that evening. He noticed that the name of the *négociant* on the label of the bottle was Gambon, the same as that on the bottle they had shared on Sunday evening, although the wine itself, a Beaujolais, was different.

'And what did you think of my piece?' she asked him impatiently while she was pouring the wine. 'You know Americans better than I do. Is this the kind of story they will be interested to read?'

'The story is fine; accurate but still interesting. Is it the first one you have written about the bishop?'

'So far, but if the *Washington Post* decides to use it, I would hope to follow it up with at least one more.'

'Do you know that Arkwright is in Paris? He is staying at the Hôtel Cheltenham.' Gautier could see no harm in telling Ingrid of Arkwright's movements. A good journalist would have been able to find them out easily enough.

Ingrid took his copy of the article and made a note at the bottom of it.

'Do you suppose he might be planning another fracas?'

'No, but one may well take place. One of his rivals in the American temperance movement is also in Paris, a Stephanie Winstock.'

'From the Women's Christian Temperance Association. I have read about her. Is she also staying at the Hôtel Cheltenham?'

'No, but Lady Jane, a good friend of hers, is. Arkwright and this Stephanie Winstock may very well meet at the hotel.'

Ingrid began pouring him another glass of wine and this gave him the opportunity to switch the conversation away from Bishop Arkwright.

'This is an excellent burgundy,' he said. 'I noticed the other evening that we were drinking a wine from the same *négociant*.'

'Gambon? Yes, a friend of mine, a member of the Gambon family was kind enough to send me a case of some of the wines they handle.'

'Was that Philippe Gambon?'

'Yes. Why? Do you know the family?'

'No, I have met Philippe Gambon once, that's all.'

'Not professionally I hope!'

Gautier was glad that her remark did not call for a reply. Ingrid knew that Bishop Arkwright had been questioned by the police over O'Flynn's murder, but he had no wish to tell her about the subsequent course of their enquiries. In any event Ingrid seemed to have no inclination to discuss the merits of the wine she had been given. Instead Gautier noticed her glancing at the clock which stood on a sideboard opposite them.

'Jean-Paul, I do not wish to seem rude,' she said, 'but I have a dinner engagement tonight.' Gautier began to rise but she checked him. 'There is no rush. Finish your wine while I go and change. Then you can escort me into the centre of Paris.'

Later that evening Gautier left Sûreté headquarters and walked along Quai des Tuileries towards the Place de la Concorde, where he would cross the river to the Left Bank. Even though it was not the most direct route to his apartment, he often chose to go that way at night, for the electric lights which had been installed in the Place de la Concorde had given the broad square and its statues a new life and vitality. For him now it really was the centre of Paris.

Earlier he had dropped Ingrid outside a restaurant in Rue la Boétie. He had never been in the restaurant himself, but over the few months since it opened it had begun to attract many of the most celebrated figures in society; the Duc and Duchesse de Greffulhe, the author Maurice Barrès and his mistress Comtesse Anna de Noailles, and Comte Robert de Montesquiou with whatever young man was his favourite at the time.

He wondered without any trace of jealousy, whom Ingrid might have been meeting at the restaurant that evening. Those of her friends whom he had met were for the most part journalists like herself and only those who wrote for the gossip columns were likely to dine in fashionable restaurants. Her own professional interests lay more in the direction of government ministers or members of the Chambre des Députés, who might provide her with material for the political column which she wrote for *Le Figaro*. He was disappointed that his evening with her had not developed in the way he had hoped, but then she had never given him any real reason for believing that it would. Intuition told him there were other evenings to come which they both would find more rewarding.

After leaving her at the restaurant, he had gone to his office, stopping only to take a cup of coffee and a cognac at a café in Place du Châtelet. The work he had to do was not onerous, mainly dealing with papers that had built up since his visit to Dijon. The statement commending Charles Dwight for his 'bravery', a copy of which had been sent to the American, was best buried in the files where the incident could be forgotten. A policeman stationed at the Gare du Nord that morning had confirmed that Benson had put the two Scottish ladies safely on to the boat train for England. Gautier felt sorry for the ladies, as the sea in The Channel was expected to be rough that day, but then perhaps a couple of hours of *mal de mer* might be a salutary lesson, reminding them that Scotch whisky, excellent drink though it might be, was best not mixed with absinthe. Gautier included a brief note on the affair in his daily report for the Director General, for, trivial though it was, Courtrand would approve of it as evidence that the Sûreté was taking good care of Anglo-Saxon visitors.

Next he went through the list of crimes which had been committed that day in Paris. Reports of major crimes which required action by the Sûreté were sent to him as well as those of all incidents involving English and American visitors. Today both lists were shorter than they normally were, but he was not naïve enough to believe that this represented a declining trend in criminal behaviour. There were many factors which might account for such a fall; for example the weather, religious holidays, even the temporary closure of a music hall habitually patronized by ruffians and prostitutes.

Even though the list was shorter than usual, reading the reports of crimes which might merit his attention had taken him until past eleven. When he arrived home work of another kind was waiting for him. The woman who came in every morning to clean his apartment had very kindly washed and pressed the clothes he had worn over the weekend. He began putting them away. As he did, he remembered his wife Suzanne. If she had not left him for another man and then died in childbirth, he might not now be living a bachelor's existence. He had never seriously thought of marrying again, even though he had been lucky enough over the years to find a succession of mistresses. Now he was beginning to accept that he never would.

Thoughts, not marriage but of sex, led him back to thinking about Ingrid. She had been married once but was now single, as well as being attractive and cultured and witty. As he tidied the apartment he resisted a temptation to fantasize and to picture what life with her would be like, for he was sure that she would never be ready to relinquish her independence. He had just put such thoughts aside when he heard a knocking on the front door of the apartment. No one, he reasoned gloomily, would rouse him at his home at that hour of night unless it was on police business. He was right. Outside the door stood a policeman who had come to tell him that a woman had been found dead in the 15th arrondissement.

'Is there no one else who could attend to the matter?' he asked the man.

'The woman is American and we have instructions that you should be informed of all crimes involving the English or Americans.'

'Where is the body?'

'In a pension where she had been staying. She was a middle-aged woman and was stabbed to death.'

'Do we know her name?'

'Yes, Chief Inspector. The owner of the pension says she was a Mademoiselle Stephanie Winstock.'

5

Although it was almost one in the morning, no one in the Pension Beau Séjour was asleep or even in their beds. The owner, dressed only in his vest and trousers, was moving around trying to reassure the guests, most of whom were standing whispering in the corridors or at the doorways to their rooms. His wife, in a dressing gown and with curlers in her hair, was in the lobby downstairs weeping, her tears interspersed with little pitiful moans. A sergeant and another policeman from the local commissariat had taken charge, but were doing nothing constructive.

The sergeant led Gautier to a bedroom on the first floor which looked as though it must be the largest in the pension as well as being the best furnished. Stephanie Winstock's body lay face up not much more than a metre from the doorway. She had been stabbed just below the throat, but the wound had not bled as much as one might have expected. The pince-nez she had been wearing had slipped from her nose and lay on the floor beside her left ear. The expression on her face seemed to be one of mild surprise rather than shock and, without the glasses which she normally wore, it looked curiously vulnerable.

'Who found the body?' Gautier asked the sergeant.

'One of the guests saw it as she passed down the corridor. The door to the room was open.'

'At what time was this?'

The sergeant shrugged. 'At least an hour ago, more probably two. The owner of the pension was reluctant to accept that the woman was dead, and as there is no telephone here he had to send a servant to the commissariat.'

'Was she sharing this room with anyone?' Gautier had noticed two single beds side by side, the covers turned down and also two night-dresses, one placed on the pillow of each bed.

'Yes, with her secretary, a Mademoiselle Pauline Fenn. No one knows where she is.'

Gautier glanced round the room which was neat and tidy. He could see nothing there which would tell one anything about the two women who had been living in it. The few personal belongings were commonplace enough; hairbrushes on the dressing-table, bedroom-slippers by the beds, a parasol standing in one corner of the room, a bible on a table between the beds; no photograph frames, no trinkets, no jewellery. He concluded that either the two women had not been there long enough to leave any traces of their personality, or that they must lead austerely simple lives. Of more relevance to Stephanie Winstock's murder, there was no sign of any dagger or knife which might have been used to stab her.

'I must speak to the owner,' he told the sergeant. 'In the meantime you and your colleague begin searching for the weapon; first here and then in the corridors and on the stairs.'

The Beau Séjour had no office as such and Gautier spoke to the owner, a Monsieur Brissart, and his wife in the living-room which they occupied. They could tell him little. Mademoiselle Winstock and her secretary had arrived there only the previous day and they understood that the ladies planned to stay for two weeks. Soon after their arrival they had visited the American embassy, but Brissart and his wife knew of no other appointments they had made. They had not seemed to behave as other foreign visitors did and gave the impression that they were in Paris on business, but had not chosen to tell anyone what that was. They were polite, well mannered and respectable.

In reply to a question from Gautier, Brissart said he had seen the Mesdemoiselles Winstock and Fenn leave the pension earlier that day and they had told him that they would be out all day. Mademoiselle Fenn returned briefly in the afternoon and was given a telegram which had arrived for her. She then went out again. One of the other guests claimed to have seen Mademoiselle Winstock returning to the pension some time before midnight, but as far as Brissart knew Mademoiselle Fenn had not yet come back.

'When Mademoiselle Winstock returned would she not have had to get a key to their room from the night porter?' Gautier asked.

'We do not have a night porter, Monsieur l'Inspecteur. Any guests intending to stay out late are requested to take the key to their room with them.'

'So Mademoiselle Fenn must have a key to their room with her?'

'Yes. At their request both ladies were given a key to the room. When we found the older lady dead her key was lying on the dressing-table in the room.' Brissart took a key from his pocket and held it up. 'I took it with me, to prevent anyone stealing it.'

When he had no more questions to ask Brissart, Gautier sent him to bring in the other guests one by one so he might question them. The majority of them were living at the pension on a semi permanent basis. They were for the most part travelling salesmen or clerks who worked in or around Paris during the week but had a home in the country to which they returned at weekends. When questioned they denied having seen or heard anything which might have a bearing on the murder and most of them had already been in bed when they were awoken by the arrival of the police. The one exception was the man who had discovered Stephanie Winstock's body. He had been passing down the corridor and, glancing through the open doorway, had seen a woman's body lying on the floor of the room. When he realized that she was dead he had called Brissart.

Having decided that there was nothing more of value he could learn from the guests at that stage, Gautier was alone, writing some notes on the murder which would be the basis of his report, when the sergeant came into the room.

'We have the woman, Chief Inspector,' he said.

'Which woman?'

'The dead woman's secretary. An officer picked her up wandering in the streets not far from here.'

'Then bring her to me.'

Pauline Fenn was younger than Gautier had expected, probably still in her twenties. She was an inch or two taller than Stephanie Winstock and not unattractive, although the pallor of her face, her crumpled clothes and untidy hair made her look wild and distraught. Gautier took her arm and helped her to a chair. He guessed that she must know her employer was dead, but decided he would test her reaction when she was told so.

'I regret to tell you, Mademoiselle, that Madame Winstock has been the victim of a tragic attack.'

Pauline Fenn looked at him calmly. 'You mean she has been murdered. I know that. You see I killed her.'

Gautier sensed that her calmness was only a façade, concealing an anguish, perhaps hysteria beneath. 'May we know why, Mademoiselle?'

'That is my affair.' Her French was fluent, with surprisingly little American accent.

'Of course, but it might help me to understand if you could explain your reasons.'

'Never!' Gautier waited for her to continue. 'She betrayed me, but that is no reason for me to do the same to her.'

'How long had you known Mademoiselle Winstock?'

'Does it matter?'

'Not really. I am just curious. You see I met her for the first time only this afternoon.'

The sergeant was still in the room with them. Gautier caught his attention and nodded in the direction of the door. He had the feeling that Pauline Fenn might be more willing to talk if they were alone. After the sergeant had left, he continued casually, 'That was not here of course, but at the Hôtel Cheltenham.'

Pauline looked at him quickly. 'Then that would have been with Lady Jane Shelford, I presume.'

'It was, yes. You know Lady Jane then?'

'Barely.' The one word was stiff with resentment. 'I was not welcome when she and Steve were alone together.'

'Did they meet often?'

'Every year, for two or three weeks in England,' Pauline replied and then she added bitterly, 'Since long before I came on the scene.'

Gautier began to feel that there was plenty this young woman would like to say and that it was only her resentment which was holding it back. If this were the case, he wondered whether there might be some way of breaching that dam and releasing her anger. Questions were clearly of no use, so he tried another angle.

'Stephanie Winstock must have been a remarkable person,' he said. 'People only speak well of her, of her intellect and acumen, of her tact and diplomacy, of her generosity and more than any thing of her unselfishness.'

'Unselfishness?' Pauline said sharply. 'Who told you that?'

'I read it,' Gautier replied, truthfully, for he had only that morning seen an article on the American Women's Temperance Union in the religious columns of one of the daily papers.

'It's nonsense! Steve used people, manipulated them.'

'Surely not?'

'I have been with her for more than two years, so I should know.' Gautier must have looked unconvinced, for Pauline continued, her voice still cold and controlled, 'For two years I have done everything for her. I have typed her letters, done her accounts, guarded her from people she did not wish to see, pressed her clothes, combed her hair, comforted her when things went badly. Oh, yes I have been much more to her than just a secretary.'

'I am sure she must have been grateful.'

'Grateful?' Her composure cracked as anger erupted. 'She betrayed me!'

'How?'

'We went to a meeting this morning and afterwards she went to a lunch to which I was not invited. In the late afternoon a telegram arrived for us at the pension with an urgent message which I knew Miss Winstock should have, so I took it round to the Hôtel Cheltenham, where I knew she must be. I was told they were dining in Lady Jane's suite. A page took me up there and what did I find?' Her lips were trembling and she could scarcely mouth the words. 'What did I find? Only that they were in bed together, making love!'

Gautier said nothing, waiting for her control to return. There were no tears, only a dry hard anger as she took a deep breath and continued; 'Can you believe that? Making love! She betrayed me!'

'Why did that shock you?' Gautier asked. 'You knew they were close friends.'

'Friends, but not lovers. I was disgusted! She deserved to die.'

Again Gautier waited. He had questions to ask her, but there might be more she would say before her self-control returned, more which would incriminate her. Presently she began to weep silently and he decided he could put the questions off no longer.

'How did you kill her, Mademoiselle?'

The question seemed to puzzle Pauline. She frowned. 'You saw her body. I stabbed her.'

'With what?'

'A knife of course.'

'Where did you get the knife?'

Pauline shook her head in irritation. 'I forget; the kitchen I suppose. Yes, that's it. I found it in the kitchen as I was waiting for Steve to return.'

'And where is the knife now?'

'I don't know. I must have taken it with me when I went out. I must have dropped it somewhere outside in the street.'

Armand Pascal was staying in a hotel, not far from the Bourse, which catered mainly for businessmen from the provinces. Finding him had not been difficult for he had registered under his own name and, as far as the police could tell, had made no attempt to conceal the fact that he was in Paris. When, on arriving at the Sûreté next morning, Gautier had been given the news, he decided he would not immediately inform Inspector Le Harivel. Pascal was not known to have committed any crime and on the two occasions when they had met Gautier had formed the impression that he was a decent enough man. The Sûrefé was not itself involved in the murder of Michael O'Flynn and it could do no harm to speak to Pascal, establish why he had come to Paris and let him know that the police in Dijon wished to question him. In Gautier's experience small courtesies like that often produced better results than clumsy attempts to demonstrate the force of the law.

When Gautier arrived at the hotel Pascal was at the concierge's desk, sending a telegram. He waited until he had finished and then approached him. Pascal seemed surprised to see him, but in no way alarmed.

'Inspector Gautier, what are you doing here?'

'I came to see you. Can you spare me a moment?'

'Of course.' Pascal looked at his pocket-watch. 'I have a business appointment, but not for half an hour.'

'In that case perhaps we might go for a stroll.'

'Willingly.'

They left the hotel together and walked down to the gardens of the Palais Royale. At that time of the morning there were few people in the arcades that ran along each side of the gardens and they could talk freely.

'I think you should be aware,' Gautier said, 'that the police in Dijon wish to speak to you in connection with the murder of Michael O'Flynn.'

'What can they possibly want? I have already told them everything I know.'

'It is probably nothing of any great consequence.'

'Surely they cannot imagine that I killed him?' Pascal began to look worried. 'He was the last person I would wish dead; in fact his death can have very serious consequences for my business.'

'In what way?'

'My vineyard is comparatively small and was very badly hit by phylloxera, so the cost of eliminating it has left us with serious debts. Michael had agreed to help me.'

Pascal explained that the solution to his difficulties was expansion. Only by buying a neighbouring vineyard and merging the two properties could the business be made viable. O'Flynn had agreed to help him finance the deal. Whether O'Flynn's widow and family would be equally helpful was, in Pascal's opinion, very doubtful.

'You may recall that when we met in Dijon on the morning after his death, I told you that I was waiting for two visitors from Paris. They were representatives of a finance house. We were to meet that morning with Michael and work out how the deal was to be financed.'

'But they never arrived in Dijon.'

'Precisely. So I came to Paris immediately, hoping to see them, but so far they have been avoiding me. That is what makes me believe that someone is trying to wreck the deal.'

'Why should they wish to do that?'

'So I would be forced to sell the vineyard, for virtually nothing. One or two firms of négociants have had their eyes on the property for some years.'

As they walked through the gardens of the Palais Royale, Pascal explained that his neighbour's vineyard, because of its similar situation, its soil and prevailing wind and weather, could easily be merged with his own. Better management would be needed and new, more modern, methods of viticulture introduced, but that need not be prohibitively costly and the owner was anxious to sell. By acquiring this other vineyard, Pascal would have almost twice the number of hectares under grapes.

'The property would still be small compared with the largest vineyards, with Château Perdrix owned by O'Flynn for example,' Pascal continued, 'but it would even so be a substantial business, producing a wine of the highest quality. Its future and that of my family would be assured.'

They walked for a while in silence, then Gautier asked him, 'When are you planning to return to Dijon?'

'Later today. My wife will already be worried at my absence.

You see I left Dijon on an impulse, in a moment of panic if you like, soon after I saw you on the morning after O'Flynn's death.'

'Then may I suggest that when you reach Dijon you contact Inspector Le Harivel as soon as possible.'

'I will of course. I have nothing to hide from him.'

After leaving Pascal, Gautier found a fiacre to drive him to the Hôtel Cheltenham. He thought it very unlikely that Lady Jane would have heard of the murder of Stephanie Winstock and felt that she should be informed of it without delay. She might also be able to give answers to some questions which were germane to the murder. When he reached the hotel he sent a page up to her suite with a message. The hotel had not yet installed telephones in the rooms of its guests, although he supposed it was only a matter of time before it did. When the page returned he told him that Lady Jane would see him in her suite in fifteen minutes.

As he waited in the hotel lobby, Gautier wondered what effect the news of Stephanie Winstock's death would have on Lady Jane. The two women were clearly close friends, but he only had Pauline Fenn's word for it that they were lovers. He was aware that there were English as well as American lesbians; some were already known to be living in Paris, where they could take advantage of the tolerant views of the French in sexual matters, but he was inclined to disbelieve what Pauline Fenn had told him. Lady Jane might well be sentimental and prone to exaggerated friendships, but she had given none of the signs of hidden passions for other women, nor if it came to that of any passion at all. He had other reasons for disbelieving what Pauline had told him at the pension and he would find out in due course whether she had been lying and why.

When eventually he was taken up to Lady Jane's suite, he found her composed, though a little irritated.

'Do you always call on people so early in the day, Inspector?' she asked him. 'I was having my breakfast when you arrived.'

'I must apologize for the inconvenience, my Lady.'

'That scoundrel has had my money for several weeks, so a few more hours will scarcely make things worse.'

'I regret to tell you that I am not here on that matter this morning, but to bring you news which I am sure will come as grave shock to you.' Gautier could see no reason for postponing what he had to tell Lady Jane. 'Mademoiselle Stephanie Winstock is dead. She was found dead last night at the pension where she was living.'

Lady Jane stared at him, the incredulity in her face being replaced first by horror and then distress. She turned pale and swayed and, afraid that she would fall, Gautier leapt forward to support her and then helped her to a chair. When the full meaning of what he was saying began to percolate into her awareness, she started stammering, expressions of disbelief, questions, grief, following each other meaninglessly. Gautier waited until the incoherence abated.

'Forgive me, Lady Jane, but there are questions I have to ask you. Firstly I understand that you and Stephanie Winstock dined together last night here in the hotel.' Lady Jane nodded, barely seeming to comprehend, so he continued, 'What time did she leave here?'

'Late. Not much before midnight I suppose.'

'Do you know how she planned to return to her pension?'

'In a fiacre. I told the concierge to send out for one.'

'Had anyone else been dining with you? Did she leave here alone?'

'No, we dined alone,' Lady Jane replied. She began to grasp the significance of Gautier's questions and looked at him wildly. 'Are you saying that someone killed her? That she was murdered? You are, are you not? I cannot believe that! There has been some terrible mistake.'

'She was stabbed to death in her bedroom at the pension.'

'By whom? Not by her secretary, surely? Pauline was devoted to Steve. She would never harm her.'

Gautier decided that he would be frank. She would learn of Pauline Fenn's admission soon enough when they both appeared before a *juge d'instruction*, if not sooner.

'Mademoiselle Fenn has admitted stabbing her employer.'

Lady Jane gasped, a short, high-pitched gasp that was more like a scream.

'I simply will not believe that! You must be mistaken. What reason could she have for killing Steve?'

'She gave me the impression that her motive must be jealousy.'

She looked at him, white faced, then buried her face in her hands.

'Oh no! Not that!' Her shoulders were shaking and Gautier wondered whether she was weeping, but if so the sobs were soundless. When she had composed herself she took her hands away from her face and looked at him. 'I was always afraid that girl would be trouble.'

He made no comment, but waited for her to continue.

Presently she said, 'Steve and I have been close friends for years but as soon as Pauline became her secretary, she began trying to possess her. She insisted on doing everything for Steve, not just secretarial duties, but personal things, combing her hair, washing her clothes, everything. And I could not help thinking that she was trying to come between us.' Again Lady Jane paused. Then she added, almost defiantly, 'I almost believe there is something unnatural in her obsession for Steve.'

Gautier had not intended to mention the reason that Pauline Fenn had given for her jealousy, but by her last remark Lady Jane had made him change his mind. She had given him an opening and it was as well that she should know of what Pauline had accused her.

'Did you know that Mademoiselle Fenn came to the hotel last night? She says she brought a message for Mademoiselle Winstock.'

Lady Jane frowned. 'That would explain the message we found in this room. She must have had it brought up by a member of the hotel staff.'

'No. She brought it up herself.'

'Then why did she not give it to Steve?'

'She says because you two were not in the room; that you were making love together in the bedroom.'

Lady Jane's reaction was not what Gautier might have expected; no confusion, no shame, no guilt, not even embarrassment. Only rage.

'Are you accusing me of unnatural sex?' she demanded angrily. 'How dare you?'

'I am accusing you of nothing, Madame.'

'This is monstrous! I will not tolerate it.'

'I am merely repeating Pauline Fenn's story, which may well be part of her defence if she is charged with murder.'

Lady Jane would not listen. 'I will not stand for this!' she shouted, rising from her chair and pointing towards the door imperiously. 'Leave this room at once or I will send for the management and have you removed.'

Gautier resisted an urge to point out to her that, although in England the aristocracy might have the power to order police officers investigating a murder out of their homes, in France the law operated differently.

'If you wish me to leave, Madame, I will. But you should know that very soon an examining magistrate will be appointed to investigate this affair. As one of the last people to see the deceased alive, you will be required to give evidence before him. I will notify you when.'

'You will not find me here,' Lady Jane replied defiantly. 'I shall return to England at once.'

'You would be unwise to try. If you do, you will be stopped and your passport confiscated. If it should prove necessary you will be detained in custody.'

Back at the Sûreté Gautier found on his desk the report of the doctor who had examined Stephanie Winstock's body. It told him little that he had not already known or guessed. She had been killed by a single downward thrust of a weapon which might have been a dagger or a sharp knife. Death had been instantaneous, suggesting that the assailant was either exceptionally skilful in handling such a weapon or very fortunate. As a rule medical examiners were apt to do no more than state the facts, but this one had tried to be helpful. The angle at which the weapon had entered the victim's body, he suggested, showed that the assailant must have been right-handed and taller than the victim, perhaps as much as twenty centimetres taller.

A copy of the report would have been sent as a matter of routine to the government laboratories, but Gautier knew that the scientists there were unlikely to add anything of value. The procedures used at the laboratory were rudimentary and the use of science as an aid to the detection of crime had made little progress since it had first been started. On leaving the pension that morning he had given instructions that a search of the streets around it should be made at first light for the weapon which had been used in the murder. So far nothing had been found. Even if the weapon were found, it would probably tell them little. The French police had recently instituted a system for the classification of fingerprints, similar to that started by the British in 1901. A 'library' of prints would take years to build up and the number so far recorded was too small to be of any practical value in crime detection.

What he needed now was to establish the timing of the murder; at what hour Pauline had arrived at the Hôtel Cheltenham with her message, when exactly she had returned to the pension; how long she had been wandering in the streets. Brissart, his wife and the guests at the pension must all be questioned again. Now that the excitement and anxiety provoked by the murder had abated and after time to reflect, they might well be able to recall facts and details which they had not mentioned earlier.

To marshal his own recollections of what had happened, Gautier took out the notes he had made at the pension and began adding to them. Eventually everything would have to be put in writing, if only to satisfy the bureaucrats. Bureaucracy was what he liked least about life in France. Napoleon had dismissed the English contemptuously as a nation of shopkeepers. In Gautier's view the French had an even greater liability; they were a nation of civil servants, of *petits fonctionnaires* who in their pedantic, demanding way governed the county.

He had written no more than a line or two when a messenger arrived to tell him that the Prefect of Police wished to see him as soon as possible. Gautier did not mind the interruption, for meetings with the Prefect were always stimulating and often led to welcome disruptions in the routine of his work.

The Prefect was a leading figure in Paris life. Immensely popular for his charm, intelligence and good humour, he had personal contacts with every politician of any importance and with many of none. His interests seemed boundless and he was seen at every race meeting at Longchamps and Auteuil, in the private boxes of the wealthy at l'Opéra and the Comédie Française and at every *vernissage* of paintings in the exclusive salons of art dealers. When he was younger he had undoubtedly been a successful womanizer and even now in his late fifties, it was rumoured, he could still seduce titled ladies old enough to know better.

The Préfecture de Police was only a short walk from Sûreté headquarters and when Gautier arrived there he was taken immediately to the Prefect's office. The Prefect was clearly in an affable mood.

'Gautier! I am glad you could come so promptly,' he said cheerfully. 'I have a suggestion to make. You are not engaged in anything too pressing, I trust.'

'Nothing that I cannot delegate, Monsieur.'

'Excellent! You were in Dijon recently, were you not?' Gautier admitted that he had been there and the Prefect continued, 'Would you be willing to go down there again?'

'Of course, Monsieur? For what purpose?'

'You may not know this, but I lived for some time in Dijon when I was a young man. A very old friend of mine, Judge Jolivet, has been appointed *juge d'instruction* for the case of a recent murder there. He will be starting his judicial examination in a day or two, but before he does, he would very much appreciate a chance to talk to you. He would value your advice on certain aspects of the case. You could easily travel down there and back in a day.'

'I would be glad to, Monsieur. When do you think I should go?'

'As soon as possible. Why not catch the first train to Dijon tomorrow morning?'

6

When Gautier arrived in Dijon the following day, he was met by Inspector Le Harivel and they walked together from the station to the Hostellerie du Chapeau Rouge. His meeting with Judge Jolivet was to be held in the hotel, because the judge wished to see exactly where O'Flynn had been murdered. The judge had already gone there and was at that moment talking to the management and examining the room which the dead man had occupied on the night of his death.

'What sort of man is Judge Jolivet?' Gautier asked Le Harivel.

'Very precise; exact. One might call him fussy. That is why he wishes to speak with you before he begins the *instruction*. He is preparing for it very thoroughly.'

'I understand the judge is a friend of our Prefect of Police.'

'At one time they were close friends. The Prefect was living in Dijon at the time. That was some years ago when I was just a boy. They say he was a popular figure here; on good terms with everyone.'

'He appears to be taking a special interest in the murder of O'Flynn.

'He knows the O'Flynn family well.' Le Harivel paused, as though wondering how much more he should tell Gautier. Then he smiled. 'People said that he and O'Flynn were rivals for the hand of a beautiful local girl, Joséphine Dubois. She chose O'Flynn and soon after, so the story goes, the Prefect moved to Paris.' Again Le Harivel paused and looked at Gautier sideways. 'Now, of course, she is a widow.'

Gautier was not sure whether there was an innuendo in Le Harivel's remark, but if there was, he was not going to pursue it. So he changed the subject.

'What about Monsieur Pascal?'

'Thanks to you, I have already spoken to him. He came to see me as soon as he returned from Paris.'

'Will he be required to give evidence at the judicial examination?'

'That will be for Judge Jolivet to decide.'

'What about Bishop Arkwright?'

'He will, certainly. After all he was staying at the hotel that night.'

'So was I.'

'But as far as we know you had no reason to wish him dead,' Le Harivel said, then he laughed. 'Did you?'

Le Harivel was developing a sense of humour, Gautier thought, always a dangerous propensity in a policeman.

When they arrived at the Hostellerie du Chapeau Rouge, they found Judge Jolivet in the room which the management had made available for their meeting, studying a sheaf of reports that he had brought with him. He was a small man, almost completely bald and with bright intelligent eyes.

'Chief Inspector!' he said, shaking Gautier's hand vigorously. 'We are most grateful to you for coming all this way.'

'It is a pleasure for me to be in Dijon again, in spite of the unfortunate circumstances which clouded my last visit. I only hope I can be of help to you.'

'You will be, I know. The first thing I would like you to do is to give me an account of everything that happened at the Château Perdrix on the evening before the homicide.'

'Everything, or just Bishop Arkwright's behaviour?'

'Everything and in detail. Inspector Le Harivel will take notes. Neither he nor I was there, you know.'

Gautier gave him a summary of all he could remember happening at the banquet and *intronisation*. From time to time the judge asked a question. The questions were all on matters which, in Gautier's view, could have no bearing on O'Flynn's murder but evidently this was the man's way of working. The case would have aroused enormous interest in Dijon and indeed in Burgundy as a whole and Jolivet was clearly determined that he would carry out his functions in a way that would be above criticism.

'What did you make of this American bishop?' Jolivet asked when Gautier had finished his account. 'Do you think he might have killed O'Flynn?'

'It is unlikely. What motive could he have had? The protest he had made at the Château Perdrix achieved what he wanted; to draw attention to himself and his cause. When he was evicted from the banquet he did not appear particularly upset. Self-important and arrogant he may be, but I do not see him as a killer.'

'My old mother always said,' Le Harivel remarked, 'that priests kill not with swords but from the pulpit.'

Next the judge began discussing the likely timing of the actual killing. The police had not been able to establish at exactly what time O'Flynn had arrived at the hotel, but the night porter who had given him the key to his room believed it was well after midnight. Bloodstains on the floor indicated that he must have been killed in his room and his body dragged into the corridor outside, where the cardinal's hat had been placed on his head.

'I have a list here of all the guests staying in the hotel that night.' Judge Jolivet held up a typewritten list. 'I think we can assume that whoever killed O'Flynn will be among them.'

'Is that wise?' Gautier asked. 'Late at night hotel porters are not always very diligent in their duties. Often they take a nap in a chair behind the reception desk. It might well have been possible for the killer to have entered the hotel unnoticed and gone up to Monsieur O'Flynn's room.'

'But if O'Flynn let him into his room, he must have known the man.'

'Or woman. Agreed.'

Their discussions did not seem to be leading to any constructive ideas, so Gautier suggested they approach the problem from a different angle. 'Perhaps we might concentrate on considering who might have had a motive for murdering Monsieur O'Flynn,' he suggested.

'The difficulty there is that I can think of no one,' the judge said. 'Michael was a reasonably popular man.'

They began discussing O'Flynn's relations with the other figures in the region's wine trade. One reason why the Château Perdrix was one of the most successful vineyards, the judge told Gautier, was its size. Because of the law of inheritance in France, many vineyards had over the years been divided into smaller and smaller units. The domaine of one of the larger châteaux might be held by as many as fifty owners, each with a tiny vineyard. In France as a whole it had been calculated that there were at least half a million families owning vineyards and in many cases these did not yield enough wine to support the owner and his family, who were therefore obliged to follow another occupation as well.

'The O'Flynn family has been fortunate. Over the last hundred years the mothers have produced plenty of daughters but few sons. One cannot say why, but as a result the family vineyard has remained large and intact. More than that, over the years it has become larger by acquiring neighbouring properties.'

'It was suggested to me,' Gautier remarked, 'that O'Flynn may have been trying to acquire the vineyard of Armand Pascal.'

'Pascal denies that,' Le Harivel said. 'He claims that O'Flynn was trying to help him raise finance to pay off his debts and to buy more land. He has given me the name of financiers in Paris whom O'Flynn had approached on his behalf.'

'Have you checked his story with the financiers?' the judge asked him.

'Not as yet.'

The judge looked at Gautier. 'Would you be prepared to do that on our behalf? Time is getting short and that would save Inspector Le Harivel having to make another trip to Paris.'

'Willingly, Monsieur le Juge.'

They continued talking about the wine trade in which Michael O'Flynn had clearly been a leading figure. Some other winemakers may have been jealous of his success and not all of them were in favour of what he was doing to raise the standard and the reputation of Burgundy wines, but neither Judge Jolivet nor Le Harivel could think of anyone who might want him dead.

'We have not talked about his family,' Gautier said. 'What family did he leave?'

'A widow and two daughters; once again no son,' the judge replied.

'Are the daughters of marriageable age?'

'Both of them have been for some time and many young men in Burgundy realize that, but so far they have made no commitments.'

When the judge had no more questions for Gautier and their meeting was over, Gautier walked to the railway station where he was told that he would have to wait for almost an hour before the next Paris train left. He was not particularly concerned and decided he could spend the time in the station restaurant taking a glass of wine and reading Duthrey's book which he had brought with him. Anything he could learn about the wines of Burgundy and those who made them might well come in useful, if he were to be consulted again by Judge Jolivet or the Dijon police. He had read no more than a page or two and had only sipped his wine, when two men approached the table at which he was sitting.

'Chief Inspector Gautier?' It was the taller and older of the men who spoke. 'May we introduce ourselves. I am Lucien Gambon and this is my son, André. Could you spare us a few minutes of your time?'

'Certainly, Monsieur.' Gautier did not wonder how the Gambons knew who he was. He would find out soon enough for it was clearly not a chance meeting.

'May we join you?' Gambon said. He was a large man with a craggy face which looked as though it had been carved out of a rough, pink marble.

'Of course. Let me offer you a glass of wine.'

'No, no. You are in our part of the world, so we must be the hosts. What are you drinking?' He took Gautier's glass and held it up to the light. 'I think we can do better than that.' He called a waiter, made him take Gautier's glass away and ordered a bottle of Château Perdrix.

When the wine had been opened and poured Gambon said, 'You will find that this is one of the best red wines in Burgundy; from the Côte d'Or; made from the pinot noir grapes which have been used by us ever since wine was first made here in the sixth century.'

'You have already met my brother Philippe, I believe,' Andre Gambon said. He was not unlike his brother in build and looks and no doubt had the same poise and self-assurance, but one had the impression that he felt slightly subdued by his father's imposing presence.

'Yes, in Paris.'

'I am told that you were at the banquet of the *Confrérie des Chevaliers du Tastevin* last week,' Gambon said.

'I was, as a guest.'

'In that case,' his father said, 'you will know about Château Perdrix. You agree, do you not, that it is a fine wine?'

'Excellent. Were either of you at the banquet?'

'No. We are first and foremost négociants-en-vins.' Then Gambon added with a self-deprecating smile, 'I suspect it will be some years before négociants are admitted to the *Confrérie*.'

'There were other négociants at the banquet,' André said to his father.

'One or two did attend,' his father agreed, 'but their invitations came only as a courtesy and not from Michael O'Flynn. Even so O'Flynn was right to start the *Confrérie*, which will be indispensable in safeguarding and promoting the reputation of wines from Burgundy.'

Gautier sensed that what the Gambons really wished to talk about was the murder of O'Flynn, but they were just skating around the subject. He decided it would do no harm to help them, for he was curious to know their views. 'If what you say is true, O'Flynn's death will be a major blow to the *Confrérie*.'

'Not only to the *Confrérie* – to the whole wine trade of Burgundy.'

'Philippe my brother says you told him you were not investigating his murder,' André said.

'That is correct. The investigation is the responsibility of the local police.'

'Then if I may ask,' Gambon said, 'why are you in Dijon today?'

'The Prefect of Police in Paris was asked if I could come down to advise the authorities here,' Gautier replied and then, thinking he might reasonably stretch the truth, he added, 'mainly on matters of procedure.'

'So the Prefect is taking an interest in the murder? I am not surprised. Dijon was his home when he was younger. A fine man.'

'He is,' Gautier agreed, 'and very able. I suppose you have not seen him for some years.'

'Oh, we have,' Gambon replied. 'He visits Dijon from time to time. In fact he has been here at least twice in the last month.'

The following morning, when Gautier reached Sûreté headquarters, he was surprised to learn that Surat was already there. He himself always arrived well before he needed to, largely because he had no family ties to keep him at home. This morning Surat was waiting outside his office and he could tell from the man's manner that he had news which he was eager to report.

'I spoke to Lady Jane yesterday as you asked me to, Patron,' he said.

'How did you find her? Difficult, no doubt.'

'Extremely awkward at first, but as we talked she gradually grew more reasonable. She was able to explain what must have happened when the American woman Pauline Fenn called at her hotel on the evening of the murder.'

'Oh yes? What did she say?'

'Apparently after your visit she checked with the hotel's concierge who confirmed that a young lady had called to see her that evening and had been shown up to her suite. If there was no one in the suite it can only have been that she and Mademoiselle Winstock were in the bedroom. They had gone in there not to make love as Mademoiselle Fenn assumed, but because Lady Jane wished to show her friend some clothes which she had bought in Paris.'

'That sounds a plausible enough story,' Gautier said.

'More plausible than that she and the stern little temperance lady should be lovers? I agree.'

'Though why she should have been so enraged when she heard what Fenn had said escapes me.'

'Because of her background no doubt. She is English and of noble birth.'

'You are to be congratulated on the way you dealt with her,' Gautier smiled as he added, 'You did much better than I.'

'She probably felt that you posed a threat to her.'

'A threat? In what way?'

Surat shrugged 'To her independence, her private life, her virginity perhaps.'

Gautier laughed. 'That is a very psychological assessment, old friend. You must be reading too many intellectual books.'

'Anyway, Patron, she regrets her outburst of temper when you went to see her. I suspect she even wishes to apologize to you.'

'Did she have any other secret thoughts which she revealed to you?'

Surat must have realized that Gautier was teasing him, but he was not going to be deflected from reporting on what he had achieved.

'Lady Jane also gave me a description of the man who persuaded her to invest in his Algerian venture. He was young, she said, tall, well mannered and clean-shaven.'

'And good looking, no doubt?'

'No, but one would not expect a middle-aged woman to admit that she had been ensnared by a handsome young man. She said nothing of his looks, but claims he told her that he had discovered the potential of Algeria while serving there as an army officer.'

'That is also plausible.'

'Is it? One would not expect an army officer to be clean-shaven.'

Gautier knew that all officers in the army, even those who were only doing their military service in the force, were obliged to have beards. Not long ago there had been the well-publicized story of a young officer whose friends had shaved off half of his beard while he was in a drunken sleep. Once awake, he had of course to shave off the other half and had then been forced to resign his commission. The disgrace had caused the young man so much anguish that he had committed suicide.

'Have you any other news for me?' Gautier was sure that Surat's handling of Lady Jane Shelford was not the only reason for his air of quiet self-satisfaction. Conscientious and loyal as he was, the man could not hide his pride whenever he had made even a minor breakthrough in the cases they were investigating.

'I have, Patron. Yesterday morning I checked the reports of the officers who had taken statements from the staff and guests at the pension on the morning after Mademoiselle Winstock's murder. I discovered that no statement had been taken from one man who had been lodging there.'

'Perhaps he left the pension early before the officers began work.'

'That should not have been possible. The previous night after you left and the American girl was taken to prison, an officer was left on duty by the door to make sure no one left the building.'

'Do we know this guest's name?'

'He registered as a Monsieur Robinet. Beyond that the owners of the pension seem to know very little about him.'

'And has he definitely left? Taken his luggage with him?'

'Yes, what little he had. I have the feeling he may have left during the night. He could easily have slipped away unnoticed in all the excitement caused by the discovery of the murdered woman's body.'

Later that morning in his office, Gautier was thinking that his visit to Dijon had meant a day wasted. He did not believe that any contribution he had made at the meeting with Judge Jolivet could have helped, either in solving the murder of O'Flynn or in the judge's handling of the *instruction*. Meanwhile there had been developments in the case of Stephanie Winstock's murder on which he himself should have acted, rather than leaving them to Surat and other officers.

Earlier, after hearing what Surat had told him, they had gone to the pension together. Their visit had been disappointing. Monsieur Robinet was apparently a Belgian and in the pension's register he had given a home address in one of the suburbs of Brussels. He had booked in to stay for just the one night and, since he appeared to be reasonably prosperous, he had been given one of the better rooms on the second floor.

'Has he ever stayed here before?' Gautier asked Brissart.

'He said he had, some months back. I did not remember him, but then we have so many casuals passing through. He said he came to us this time because he could not get a room at his usual hotel.'

'Which hotel was that?'

'He did not say.'

'What sort of age was he?'

'In his forties, I would say, but he looked older. Both his hair and his beard were shot with grey.'

No one at the pension apart from Brissart had actually spoken to Monsieur Robinet and no one else could describe him. This had not surprised Gautier, as he had found that people in general were not observant and paid no attention to any one individual unless they had a reason for doing so. Robinet, he had been told, had paid for his room on arrival at the pension and was therefore free to leave at whatever time suited him.

'There was one odd thing,' Brissart had told Gautier, 'his bed had not been slept in that night. Either that or he remade it before he left.'

He and Surat had returned to the Sûreté where Surat was now putting routine measures in train to see whether this Robinet could be traced. A message had been telegraphed to the police in Brussels asking them if anyone of that name was known at the address he had given. Meanwhile similar enquiries would be made in small hotels and pensions in Paris, but Gautier was not very hopeful that they would produce results.

After clearing the day's work that had accumulated on his desk, he set out for the Café Corneille. His route took him past the bank of the Seine opposite to Sûreté headquarters, along which the *bouquinistes* had their stalls of second-hand books. Sometimes he would stop and browse among the books, but today he had other thoughts on his mind and he was surprised when he saw his friend Duthrey standing in front of one of the stalls, talking to the *bouquiniste*. Duthrey was a man of fastidious tastes who set great value on the appearance of books and one would never associated him with anything second-hand. As Gautier approached them the *bouquinste* handed Duthrey a book which he had wrapped in brown paper.

'Duthrey, old friend, what bargain of a forgotten classic have you picked up today?' he called out.

'Nothing of any consequence,' Duthrey said brusquely. Then, thinking some further explanation was required he added, 'It is just a novel that my wife wishes to read and which is out of print.'

He was clearly embarrassed that his friend should have found him by the bookstalls and suddenly Gautier guessed why. His book on wine had been published several weeks previously and discarded copies might well now be available. He must be one of those authors who could not bear that his *chef d'oeuvre* should suffer the indignity of being exposed at a greatly reduced price among other trivial and often salacious works. It was only vanity but, as Gautier knew, everyone was entitled to their own vanities.

They set out for the Café Corneille together, which suited Gautier as he wished to discuss a matter which he would prefer not to raise at the café.

'A day or two ago,' he said, 'I met a Lucien Gambon who is connected with the wine trade in Burgundy. Have you ever heard of him?'

'The *négociant*? Oh, yes. His is a well established business on the Côte d'Or.'

'What does a *négociant* do? Sell wines?'

'There is much more to it than that. Without *négociants* many of the wines of France would never reach our tables at home, much less those of wine drinkers overseas. Not only do the *négociants* buy the wine produced at scores of small vineyards, but in many cases they provide the capital needed to bottle it, to age it and sell it to customers. The name of a reliable *négociant* on a label is a guarantee of good quality.'

'And you say that Gambon is reliable?'

'Totally, as far as the wines he ships arc concerned.'

Gautier hesitated before making his next remark, for he knew Duthrey was still sensitive on the subject of the *Chevaliers du Tastevin*. 'Yet he was not invited to the banquet at the Château Perdrix.'

'In my view he should have been by right, for he is a man of good standing on the Côte d'Or. Frankly though, not everyone in the wine trade trusts him. Gambon is ambitious, some say too ambitious. He began as a *courtier*.'

Duthrey explained that a *courtier* was a wine-broker, who acted as a middleman between producers and the *négociant*, taking a percentage of any deals he arranged. The craft was an ancient one, formally recognized by the establishment of the *Corps de Courtiers* in the fifteenth century. *Courtiers* had to have an immense knowledge of wine as well as an innate flair for assessing its quality.

'Now Gambon is a sound, well-established *négociant*, but he is not satisfied with that. He has already bought a small vineyard for his elder son André and has his eyes on others. The family would like to possess its own wine-growing château and I have no doubt that in the course of time that will come about.'

By this time Gautier and Duthrey had arrived at the Café Corneille. Some of their friends were already there and the conversation was not about wine this time but about the murder of Stephanie Winstock. Her murder had created something of a sensation in Paris, not for how and where it had been committed but for its connection with the activities of the American temperance movement.

'One must feel sorry for the woman,' Froissart was saying. 'In spite of her views, she never did anyone harm.'

'I feel almost guilty,' the deputy for Seine-et-Marne told the others. 'The last time her name was mentioned here I attacked her scathingly for trying to interfere with our French way of life. I had no idea that anyone felt strongly enough to kill her.'

'The motive for her murder does not appear to have been political,' the elderly judge said. 'They are saying she was killed by her secretary, for whom she had a lesbian attachment.'

'Speculation is futile,' Froissart told him. 'We will learn the truth soon enough.'

The others in the group fell silent for a time. There was an unspoken convention that they did not raise any matter which might embarrass one of their number and in this case the courtesy was for Gautier. He responded by quickly introducing a new subject for discussion, drawing their attention to a rumour, not yet confirmed, that Sarah Bernhardt, recognized as the greatest actress in France, had announced her retirement from the stage.

'No one will believe her,' Duthrey protested. 'How many times have we heard this before?'

'She said her last year's tour of America was to be her last.'

'I have it on good authority,' the elderly judge told the others, 'that she has agreed to appear in Richepin's new play *La Belle au Bois Dormant* later this year.'

'What part is she to play?'

'Prince Charming of course. She loves male parts.'

'But she is over sixty!'

'Sixty-three, even if you believe what she claims was her date of birth.'

Sarah Bernhardt was a good subject for a lively and topical discussion. Her eccentricities, her pet monkeys, the crocodile she was said to have admitted to her bed, her love affairs and disastrous marriage to a morphine addict, the rumours, many of which she had started herself, all provided material to shock and amuse. Beneath all the badinage, though, one could sense the very real affection in which she was held by everyone at the café that day. Only when they had left the café together and were heading down the Boulevard St Germain, did Gautier have an opportunity to ask Duthrey one last question.

'What will happen to the Château Perdrix? I understand O'Flynn left no sons.'

'His widow will inherit the property. After that. . . ?'

Duthrey shrugged and Gautier wondered what he should read into the shrug. When he was writing his book on the wines of Burgundy, Duthrey must have met or corresponded with O'Flynn on a number of occasions, for it contained information about Château Perdrix which he could only have obtained at first hand. Intuition told Gautier that the affairs of the O'Flynn family might hold a clue to the murder of Michael O'Flynn and what happened subsequently.

'Is it possible that one of his two daughters will inherit the château if she were to marry?' he asked.

Duthrey did not answer the question directly. 'Oh, they will both marry. Both are attractive, both wealthy in their own right. They would have married before if their father had not been over-protective. It must have been the Irish blood in him, but he turned away any number of suitors.'

'And will their mother now encourage them to marry?'

'Why not? She surely will not want them to stay on at home indefinitely. Moreover I believe that for some time Madame O'Flynn has been bored with life in Burgundy. Incomprehensible though it may seem, she would like to escape from the provinces and live in Paris, enjoy society here at the highest level, go to the theatre and the opera, eat in fashionable restaurants.'

'And drink wines better than those from the family château?'

'Indeed.'

7

Chéri,

If you have nothing more important to do, could we meet this evening? Not for dinner as I already have a dinner engagement, but afterwards at the Hôtel Cheltenham. Do come if you possibly can as you may not be seeing me again for some time. Shall we say ten o'clock?

Ingrid.

The note had come in a *petit bleu* or message sent by Paris's pneumatic telegraph and was waiting on Gautier's desk when he returned from the Café Corneille. It intrigued him on two counts, as no doubt it was intended to. The first was why she wished to meet at the Hôtel Cheltenham. Did that mean she was dining at the hotel and if so could that mean she was dining with Bishop Arkwright? She had already written a newspaper article on the bishop and one way of collecting material for another would be to interview him. The second thing in her note that made him curious was her reference to the fact that he would not be seeing her for some time. He knew she was the Paris correspondent for a German newspaper and he wondered whether she had been recalled to Leipzig for some reason.

His speculation was brought to an end when Surat came in to

report on the enquiries which he and other officers had been making that morning. First was the news – or lack of it – about Robinet. The Brussels police had found no one of that name at the address entered in the register of the Pension Beau Séjour, nor was any Robinet known to the Belgian police. A more positive result was that the weapon used to stab Stephanie Winstock had been found. It was not a knife but a dagger of curious shape and old enough to be a museum piece. An expert on swords and daggers was studying it in the hope that he might be able to identify it more precisely. but there was little doubt that it was the murder weapon. It had been concealed under the carpet in the room next to the one occupied by Stephanie Winstock and Pauline Fenn and both it and the carpet were stained with blood. It should have been found earlier when the pension was being searched by the police, but the delay was not likely to cause any problems.

On a different issue, Surat had that morning visited the bank that Pascal claimed had been advising him on the restructuring of his debts and on making his vineyard into a viable business. Two members of the bank's staff had confirmed Pascal's story. They agreed that they had intended to travel down to Dijon for a meeting with Pascal and O'Flynn, but said that there had been some confusion over the dates of their visit, which was why they had not appeared on the morning after O'Flynn's murder. After telling Gautier the facts, Surat went to telegraph the information to Inspector Le Harivel in Dijon.

When Surat had left, Gautier had the best part of an hour to catch up with odd pieces of work left over from the day he had spent in Dijon, before the meeting which he had arranged for that afternoon was due to start. One of the two people coming to the meeting was Pauline Fenn, who was being brought to Sûreté headquarters from the prison in which she had been lodged since she had been arrested. When she arrived, escorted by two woman prison-warders, he could see at once the effect of her stay in prison. There she would have spent the nights herded into a cell with perhaps as many as twelve thieves, drunkards or prostitutes. For a young woman of her background it would have been a harrowing experience. At their first meeting and from the appearance of her bedroom at the pension, he had formed an impression that she was a methodical young woman proud, perhaps too proud, of her neat appearance and of the orderly way she looked after her employer and herself. Now, while one could not say that she looked dirty, her hair hung down, straight and dank, her clothes seemed bedraggled, her back bowed. Gautier led her to a chair and told the warders to leave.

'Why have I been brought here?' she asked with just a hint of defiance.

'Officials from the American embassy wish to assure themselves that you are being properly treated. They could have visited you in prison, but I thought it better if they spoke to you in my office. One of them will be here directly.'

'I do not wish to be given any favours.'

'You certainly will not be given any if you persist in saying that you killed Mademoiselle Stephanie Winstock.'

'I did.'

'Lady Jane's account of what happened when you called at her suite in the Hôtel Cheltenham is very different from yours.'

'Does she deny that she and Steve were in her bedroom?'

'No.'

Gautier decided he would not give her Lady Jane's explanation of what happened that evening. Pauline was so consumed by jealousy, that by now she probably believed that she had seen Lady Jane Shelford and Stephanie Winstock in bed together. Anyway he had a better way of testing her confession to murder.

So he began questioning her on a different matter, on her life in America and how she had come to be working as Stephanie Winstock's secretary. She answered grudgingly and he had not progressed very far when Ferry, a junior official from the American embassy, was shown into the room. The embassy had already been informed of Pauline Fenn's arrest and the ambassador was unhappy that she should be held in prison, but recognized that in view of her confession, prison was inevitable.

When he saw Pauline in the room, Ferry looked uneasy. He did not seem entirely sure of how he should greet her and nodded stiffly in what one supposed was intended as a formal bow, before asking after her health and well-being. Gautier wondered whether the decision to send a relatively junior official to meet Pauline that afternoon was an indication that the embassy itself did not wish to get too closely involved in a murder which might be in some way associated with a lesbian attachment. He waited until Ferry had asked his questions before intervening.

'Monsieur Ferry,' he said, 'would you mind if I asked Mademoiselle Fenn one or two questions in your presence? There are some matters which need to be resolved.'

'No, Inspector, of course not.'

'Mademoiselle, when I asked you on the night of your employer's murder, you told me you had stabbed her with a knife.'

'That is correct.'

'You also said that you had found the knife in the kitchen of the pension and that subsequently you must have dropped it in the street when you went out.'

Pauline looked at him sullenly. 'Yes.'

'I have to tell you that we have found the weapon which was used to kill Mademoiselle Winstock. It was not a knife, but a dagger of a very distinctive shape. Moreover it was not found in the streets but hidden in a room at the pension.'

'Knife, dagger. What does it matter?' Pauline shouted angrily. 'I tell you I killed her and she deserved to die.'

Ferry, who had been watching Pauline as the argument developed, looked puzzled. He said to Gautier, 'Inspector, what is the purpose of these questions, may I ask?'

'Monsieur, from the outset I found it hard to believe that Mademoiselle killed the woman whom she loved and whom she had served so devotedly. From what we know now, it is clear that she did not.'

'Then what do you want from her?'

'An admission that she was not the murderer.' Gautier turned to Pauline. 'Mademoiselle, you keep saying that Stephanie Winstock deserved to die. That is not true. She was a good woman, sincere and kind who was brutally and callously killed. Do you not want her killer brought to justice? By your false confession you are only hindering us. Please, I beg you to reconsider and to help us!'

Pauline stared at him, her expression unchanging. Then suddenly her defiance collapsed. She buried her face in her hands and began to weep, soundlessly at first and then with huge, convulsive sobs.

Ferry was clearly moved by her distress. He rose from his chair, went across to Pauline, placed his arm around her shoulders, trying to comfort her.

'Inspector,' he said to Gautier, 'if Miss Fenn retracts her confession, admits that she did not kill Stephanie Winstock, would she be freed?'

'She would be released from prison certainly. As to being free, she could not of course leave the country, for she is in effect a witness and will have to be questioned by the examining magistrate. Your embassy would have to give us certain guarantees.'

Pauline looked up. 'I could not return to the pension,' she said between her sobs. 'I could not bear that!'

'Of course not, my dear,' Ferry said. 'You can come to stay with my wife and me in our apartment. We will look after you. Just admit you did not murder your employer.'

Pauline looked at Gautier, her tears drying up as a measure of composure returned. 'Of course I did not kill Steve. How could I have done? I loved her more than anyone, more than life itself, more than I love God!'

'I have to say, Gautier, that I am not happy with the way your investigation into the death of this American woman is proceeding.' Courtrand held up the copy of the report which had been placed on his desk earlier that morning.

'Why do you say that, Monsieur?'

'For several reasons. What disquiets me most is that the story of these two women being in bed together may become public knowledge. Think what that will do to the reputation of France! I accept that we French are liberal in matters of sex, that is why King Edward and so many English gentlemen come to Paris, knowing that they can escape the ridiculous taboos of London society. But that is normal. Lesbians are not welcome here.'

Gautier supposed it was just possible that Courtrand might be one of the few people who were unaware of the colony of lesbians, many of them poets, writers and artists, which had formed itself in Paris where it could take advantage of the liberal attitude to sex which prevailed in society. So he made no comment. Instead he said, 'There have been new developments in this affair, Monsieur.'

'What developments?'

Gautier told him of the meeting which had just concluded and that Pauline Fenn had retracted her confession.

Courtrand listened and then he asked, 'Does this mean that the girl will also withdraw her accusations against the English milady?'

'Let us say I believe she accepts that she may have been mistaken.' Gautier felt he was safe in making that assumption.

'Good! You see, Gautier, you were right in bringing in the American embassy; in fact you should have called on their help much sooner. How many times have I told you that diplomacy is our most valuable weapon in our fight against crime? Who did the embassy send to your meeting?'

'A Monsieur Ferry, he is a fairly junior official.'

'A junior official?' Courtrand could not hide his disappointment. 'Ah, well! We may still have to take the matter higher. Let me know if you would like me to have a word with the ambassador.' Gautier turned to leave the room, but Courtrand had more to say. 'There is one more thing, Gautier. I have a message for you from the Prefect of Police. Would you go and see him in his office as soon as possible.'

'Of course. I will go at once, Monsieur.'

'I do not imagine it is all that urgent.'

Gautier was aware that Courtrand was suspicious of his relationship with the Prefect, who had made it clear that he recognized Gautier's ability and had more than once defended him when Courtrand was proving difficult.

'I have no idea what the Prefect can possibly want,' Courtrand added. 'I suppose he has some favour to ask of us. You will keep me informed, Gautier, will you not?'

Gautier left Sûreté headquarters and went directly to the Prefecture, where he found the Prefect waiting for him. When Gautier arrived the Prefect looked up at the clock which hung on one wall of the room and a trace of anxiety might have been detected below his usual confident bonhomie. Another possible sign of anxiety was that he did not waste time on courtesies, but began straight away to explain why he had sent for Gautier.

'Are you free tomorrow afternoon? In fact if you are not, you must make the time. A lady whom I know wishes to see you on a delicate matter of some importance.'

'May I know her name, Monsieur?'

'It is better at this stage if you do not. You will guess who she is when you meet her, but I am not going to give you her name now, nor tell you why she wishes to speak with you. She would like you to meet her at three-thirty tomorrow at my club.'

'The Cercle Angevin?'

Although in general the French tended to be scornful of the English, that had not stopped them from imitating the habits, manners and institutions of English society. One of these was the gentleman's club. Membership of Paris's Jockey Club carried a special cachet and almost equally exclusive was the Cercle de la rue Royale. The Cercle Angevin, to which the Prefect of Police belonged, might be thought to be less distinguished, but its members, drawn from senior members of the administration, carried in their own way more influence than the *princes*, *ducs* and *comtes* of other clubs. Its full name was *Le Cercle des Chevaliers d'Anjou*, taken from an ancient and long-forgotten order of chivalry, but members now felt that an abbreviated version was more discreet.

'You have been to my club,' the Prefect continued, 'and may be surprised that I am asking you to meet a lady there. The reason is that I could think of nowhere else where you two could meet with complete discretion, one might even say in secrecy. No members are likely to be in the premises on a Saturday afternoon and I have made special arrangements which should prevent anyone knowing that a lady is there.'

'You can rely on me to be discreet.'

'One more thing. The lady is likely be in heavy mourning.'

When Gautier arrived at the Hôtel Cheltenham he was shown into the manager's office. His friendship with the manager, Pierre Desportes, dated back some years to a time when Gautier had been able to save the hotel unwelcome publicity after an English visitor had been murdered there. The friendship had been useful to him on more than one occasion, in particular when he had spent a night at the hotel with one of his mistresses and the management had not only looked the other way, but had forgotten to give him a bill.

That evening, after a solitary dinner at the café in Place Dauphine, he had gone to the hotel well before the time of his rendez-vous with Ingrid, hoping that he might learn whether Bishop Arkwright had been causing any trouble at the hotel. He had warned Desportes that he would be coming and when he arrived they met in the manager's office, where he accepted a glass of cognac. On his way to the office he had passed the hotel's dining-room, where he had seen that Ingrid was dining with the bishop and Mrs Barclay.

'Tell me,' he said to Desportes after they had chatted for a time. 'You have an American bishop staying here. I wondered whether he might have been causing the hotel any problems.'

Desportes laughed. 'On his first evening here he went round the dining-room, warning the other guests that they were selling their souls to the devil by drinking wine. Most people merely laughed at him, but on the second night we began to get complaints. I had to tell him and his lady-friend that if he did not restrain himself they would be asked to leave the hotel. Since then we have had no trouble.'

'Are he and his friend Mrs Barclay sharing a room?'

'Certainly not.' Desportes lifted his eyes to the roof in mock alarm. 'Think of it! If we had allowed a bishop to live here in sin with a mistress the hotel's reputation would be ruined. On the other hand we would probably become much more popular with foreigners. No, Mrs Barclay is not his mistress, she is sponsoring his visit to Europe.'

'Do you know how long they plan to stay?'

'They have not given a date. I thought they might have wished to leave when they heard that an American lady was murdered after calling on a friend here at the hotel. A murder even remotely connected with a hotel always makes guests uneasy. But these two have not even mentioned it.'

'As you must have realized, we are investigating that murder. Stephanie Winstock represented a different organization in the American temperance movement from the one which the bishop supports. They were bitter rivals and it is unlikely that he would be too upset by her death.'

'That does not surprise me, knowing the man.'

'I had to give Lady Jane the news that Winstock had been murdered. It came as a terrible shock to her.'

'So it seems. She is still distraught. Never leaves her suite, has all her meals sent up, eats virtually nothing and seems to take no trouble with her appearance.'

Gautier had an idea. Ingrid and Bishop Arkwright were still only half-way through their dinner, so he had time to spare. 'I wonder whether she might be willing to see me. Could you arrange for a note to be sent up to her suite?'

'Certainly.'

Taking a sheet of notepaper which Desportes gave him, Gautier wrote on it,

Mademoiselle,

I happen to be in the hotel this evening and wondered if you would allow me to call on you to pay my respects. I hasten to say that this is not an official visit, but I have news which will be of interest to you.

Jean-Paul Gautier

Desportes sent for the concierge, who took the note and sent a page up with it to Lady Jane. They did not have long to wait for the reply, which was that Lady Jane Shelford would be willing to see Inspector Gautier in her suite if he would be kind enough to wait for ten minutes.

'She wishes to beautify herself for you,' Desportes said, teasing.

When he was admitted to her suite, Gautier wondered whether Desportes might have been right, for Lady Jane seemed to have made an effort to make herself look, if not beautiful, then at least presentable. Her hair had been brushed and tied back and she had used cosmetics, not very skilfully, to conceal the pallor of her face. She gave Gautier a wan smile and held out her hand to be kissed.

'I owe you an apology, Inspector,' she said. 'I treated you with unreasonable harshness the other day.'

'It was my misfortune to bring you news which was so painful to you.'

'You mentioned in your note that you have more news for me today. Let us hope it is not equally distressing.'

'It concerns Mademoiselle Pauline Fenn. As you know she told us that it was she who had stabbed Mademoiselle Winstock. She has now admitted that that was not the truth.'

'Thank heavens for that!' Lady Jane paused and looked at Gautier. He guessed what she might be thinking. 'And what about that other tale she was telling? Has she withdrawn that as well?'

'In my view she came to the hotel that evening so consumed by jealousy that she might have said anything. She may even have been looking for some way of discrediting you. No, what

Mademoiselle Fenn said about that evening can safely be forgotten.'

'Poor thing! One can understand what she must be feeling.'

Remembering Lady Jane's outburst and her rage when he had first told her of the accusation that Pauline Fenn had made, Gautier was surprised at her composure now. Her grief over Stephanie Winstock's death had been genuine, he was sure of that, but now she could talk rationally about what had happened and could even show some sympathy for the woman who had slandered her. This he supposed might be an effort of self-control, the discipline instilled in the English by an upbringing which was so foreign to the emotional French.

She had one more question to ask him. 'Have you any idea, Inspector, of when I will be allowed to return to England?'

Gautier told her that in all probability a *juge d'instruction* would be appointed on Monday of next week and would begin his work at once. He would arrange that Lady Jane should be one of the first witnesses to appear before him, after which he was sure she would be free to go home.

She sighed. 'I do hope so! After what has happened I am dreading staying on here alone, particularly over the weekend.'

When he was returning to the manager's office, Gautier saw that Ingrid was still in the dining-room with Bishop Arkwright and Mrs Barclay. He also noticed that the hotel's concierge was at his desk. He went to have a word with the man who, he learnt, had been on duty on the evening when Stephanie Winstock had been murdered.

The concierge confirmed that Mademoiselle Winstock had left the hotel that evening soon after 11.30.

'You are sure of that?' Gautier asked him.

'Quite sure, Chief Inspector. It is unusual for single ladies to be leaving the hotel alone at that time. I sent a page out to find a fiacre for her. He had difficulty in finding one and finally had to wait until one arrived bringing another American lady back to the hotel.'

'Who was that?'

'Madame Barclay.'

'Was Bishop Arkwright with her?'

'No, she was alone.'

Ingrid seldom travelled alone at night in a fiacre. Her work as a journalist often took her out late, so she had recently made an arrangement with a company which hired out carriages, whereby she could be driven from her apartment and back again whenever she needed it. She explained this to Gautier as they were leaving the Hôtel Cheltenham together.

'How kind of you to wait,' she said. 'The bishop seemed to be in no hurry to get to bed and in the end Mrs Barclay went upstairs and left us alone together.'

'What sort of woman is she?'

'Charming. She is paying for his visit to Europe, you know.'

'I hope she is getting value for her money.'

'I am sure she is.' Ingrid leant over in the darkness of the carriage and kissed him lightly on the cheek.

'Is she also an apostle of temperance?'

'Not a very devoted one, in my opinion. She let me know that she does take a glass from time to time, but not when she is with him in public.'

She kissed him again, rather more seriously this time. Gautier had often read in novels of people making love in carriages, but theirs was moving at a brisk speed over cobbled streets and he could not help feeling that any strenuous display of passion might be risky, so he decided to take Ingrid at her word and wait in expectation, as it were.

'You said in your note that I might not be seeing you for some time,' he said. 'Why is that?'

'I have to go to Washington.'

'When?'

'Tomorrow.'

Ingrid explained that on the basis of the articles she had been sending to it, the paper planned to offer her some sort of contract, but wished to meet her first. So she had been asked to go over to the States as soon as possible. She had managed to book a passage on a liner which was due to sail from Cherbourg the following afternoon.

'This is exactly what I have been hoping for,' she said.

'I trust this will not mean that you will be moving out of my life,' Gautier said lightly.

'On the contrary. It may well end up by being exactly the opposite.'

She made no attempt to explain her cryptic remark and Gautier decided not to ask her what she meant. There would be time enough to play word-games when she returned from America. In any event shortly afterwards the carriage came to a halt outside her home. Once they were inside the apartment, she did not waste time on words either, but led him straight to her bedroom and began taking off her clothes. He had been expecting that she would make at least a token show of seducing him, but any surprise he might have felt was soon engulfed in a mounting wave of excitement.

Her body was even more inviting than he had imagined it might be, her breasts firm, her stomach flat, her thighs slim but compelling when she wound them round him. She made love fiercely, with the same directness typical of the way she spoke, argued, laughed. When the first passion was spent, they lay back and talked, but not about the love they had shared, nor even of themselves. Gautier could tell that her mind was engrossed with America and the adventure which would begin the next day.

'What did you learn about Bishop Arkwright this evening?' he asked her.

'Not enough for another article on him yet. He is an odious man, ambitious, ruthless and a bigot. He loathes Catholics, blaming them for all the drunkenness and sin in America. Equally he hates Germans, who own most of the breweries in the States, and Italians for giving Americans a taste for wine. When he learnt that I was Dutch and not a Catholic, he warmed towards me, if one can use that expression for anyone as cold as he.'

'In your opinion could he have murdered Stephanie Winstock?'

'Never. He is a bully and a braggart, but he would not have the courage.'

Ingrid turned, propped herself on one arm and looked at him. 'I am going to miss you while I am away.'

'I cannot believe that! Your life is too well organized, too complete. I have the feeling you are self-sufficient.'

'How wrong you are! I need a man. I need you.' She put an arm round his shoulders and pulled him towards her. 'And not only for the moment.'

They made love again with her astride him this time. The passion, though less fierce and more leisurely, was equally intense. When it ended she lay back, her head on his shoulder.

'Shall I leave you now?' he asked.

'No, stay the night.' She laughed. 'In the morning you can help me pack.'

8

Next morning through the post Gautier received an invitation to a dégustation or tasting of wines from Burgundy. The invitation was printed on both sides of a gilt edged card, in French on one side and in English on the other. The English version read:

Philippe Gambon
on behalf of Lucien Gambon et fils
takes pleasure in inviting
Monsieur Jean-Paul Gautier and guest to
a tasting of fine wines from Burgundy
to be held in the Salle Delacroix.

The tasting was to be held the following Tuesday at 6 p.m. Monsieur Gautier was requested that, if he intended to take a guest to the tasting, would he be kind enough to telephone the Salle Delacroix in advance so that the guest's name could be added to the list of those invited.

Gautier knew that the Salle Delacroix was in the Avenue de Marigny, just off the Champs Elysées. It had been built only a year or two ago, primarily as a lavish art gallery but it could also be hired for receptions. Since it had become a popular venue for events in the social calendar of Paris, one might assume that the wine-tasting had been arranged some weeks previously. Gautier wondered why the tasting had not been cancelled as a token of respect for the memory of Michael O'Flynn, but then he reflected that O'Flynn's death had made little impact in Paris. The tasting must be part of Gambon's marketing plans for the wines he sold and one could understand why he would be reluctant to abandon it. The realities of commercial life must be accepted.

Soon after he had put the invitation aside, he received another envelope which had been delivered to Sûreté headquarters by hand and which he saw had come from the American Embassy. Before handing Pauline Fenn over to the embassy, he had suggested to her that she should prepare herself for the questioning to which she would be submitted by the *juge d'instruction*. She and her employer had arrived in France only a short time before the murder and it seemed probable that Stephanie Winstock had been attacked by someone who had followed her to Paris, or whom she had met there after her arrival.

The judge was likely to ask Pauline to tell him everything they had done after their arrival and everyone whom they had met. Gautier could see now that she had decided to anticipate such a question and had prepared a detailed account of how they had spent the two days. It was written in longhand in the practical but inelegant script which he recognized as typical of that used by many Americans.

FOR INSPECTOR GAUTIER

Account of days spent in Paris by S. Winstock (deceased) and P. Fenn.

Day One: We arrived in Paris by train from Cherbourg in the afternoon and went directly to the pension where I had previously booked accommodation for the two of us. We were pleased with the room we were given, which was clean and comfortable and as we were tired after the journey, we lay down for a rest, only waking in time to go out and have a meal in a nearby café.

Day Two: The main purpose of Miss Winstock's visit to Paris was to expedite the formation of a French branch of the American Women's Temperance Association. For some months we had been corresponding with several French ladies, who were prepared to become involved in such a project and meetings had been arranged with three of their number. The first of these took place on the morning of the second day of our visit. (I can supply the names of these three ladies, who are all of strong religious convictions and the highest probity.) A further meeting was planned for later in the week, when more ladies were to be present and officers elected to run the new organization. Prior to this first meeting Miss Winstock and I had paid a brief courtesy visit to the American Embassy in Paris, where we were made welcome by an official, a Mr Ferry. We met no other officials there, nor anyone else on this, the first morning of our stay.

Miss Winstock had known for some time that a very close English friend of hers, Lady Jane Shelford, was to be in Paris at the same time as we were and had planned that they would meet. Unfortunately our departure from the United States had unexpectedly been brought forward and as a result we sailed before receiving a letter from Lady Jane, from which we would have learnt the name of the hotel in Paris where she would be staying.

Miss Winstock was in no way dismayed by this contretemps and was confident that she would soon be able to locate the hotel where her ladyship would be staying. She appeared to believe that there were only three or four hotels in Paris that catered for English visitors.

So in the afternoon of our second day she decided to visit each of these hotels in turn to find out whether Lady Jane was staying there. I suggested that it would be easier of she were to telephone the hotels, but she would have none of it. Miss Winstock was remarkably naïve for a woman of her age and she could not resist the excitement of looking for her friend, finding and surprising her. Before setting out on her search, she even changed from the formal costume she had been wearing that morning into an outfit which she considered – wrongly in my view – to be more seductive.

After she had left I remained at the pension, preparing a report on our morning's meeting to be mailed to A.W.T.A. headquarters in the States. Later that afternoon a telegram arrived for us at the pension, containing important news which meant that *inter alia* we would have to change the itinerary of our journey in Europe and our travelling arrangements. I realized that Miss Winstock must be informed as soon as possible. Accordingly I did what she should have done earlier and telephoned the hotels on her list, I learnt that Lady Jane was staying at the Hôtel Cheltenham and that she was entertaining an American visitor, who I guessed could only be Steve.

It was early evening when I arrived at the hotel and was taken up by a page to Lady Jane Shelford's suite. When we went into the drawing-room of the suite there was no one inside, but I could hear voices coming? from the bedroom. As I felt I had no right to interrupt whatever Steve and Lady Jane might be doing, I left the telegram where they would find it and left.

With nothing else to do, I decided to stroll through Paris and see some of the sights for which I knew the city was famous. This was, after all, my first visit, although Steve had been there before. I met no one and spoke to no one during my stroll. On two or three occasions passing men called out to me with what I suppose were invitations – that is one of the disgusting habits of Europeans – and I ignored them. Eventually, realizing that Steve and Lady Jane must be dining together, leaving me to my own devices for the evening, I crossed to the Left Bank, had my dinner at a small café and continued my sight-seeing in Paris. It must have been close on midnight when I returned to our pension. I went to our room, opened the door with my key and saw Steve lying on the floor dead.

I cannot recall my movements immediately after finding her body. In my shock and horror I must have rushed from the room and out of the building. I remember deciding to stay near the pension. I could not accept the fact that Steve was dead and thought that it had all been a terrible dream and that if I watched the entrance to the pension, I would see her return. Some time later, I do not know how long, a policeman found me and took me back to the pension. From there I was taken to prison.

This is a truthful account of all I can remember of my days in Paris and I would be willing to swear a deposition on oath to that effect.

Signed: Pauline Lucy Fenn (spinster)

Gautier read the statement through for a second time. One could see that even now Pauline Fenn had not rid herself of her jealousy towards Lady Jane and her resentment of the way in which Stephanie Winstock had treated her. She had not been able to refrain from little spiteful comments on Stephanie's naïveté and on her attempts to improve her appearance. Although the statement, which may well have been accurate and true, gave an indication of Pauline's state of mind, it offered little help in the investigation of Stephanie Winstock's murder.

He sent for Surat and handed him Pauline Fenn's account. When Surat had finished reading it, Gautier said, 'I suppose it might just be worthwhile checking at the hotels which Mademoiselle Winstock may have visited when she was searching for Lady Jane.'

Surat looked doubtful. 'You believe she may have met, or been seen by, a stranger at one of the hotels or become involved in some incident which may have resulted in her being murdered?'

'It is unlikely, I agree, but at the moment I can think of no other avenues we might explore. I understand she knew few people in Paris.'

The Cercle Angevin was in an obscure street off the Rue La Boétie, its entrance concealed behind large wooden doors, which were usually kept closed. Beyond the doors was a courtyard overlooked by the building which housed the club's premises and which had an air of bleak anonymity. It required a feat of imagination to believe that behind those walls men of power met and exchanged social courtesies or, from time to time, contrived secret plots to safeguard the administration of France. Discretion was the first aim of the members and Gautier had to concede that they had achieved their purpose.

When he arrived at the club the following afternoon he was met by the chief steward and taken to a room at the back of the building where informal committee meetings were held. Like the other rooms it was furnished in a style that was almost a parody of rooms in gentlemen's clubs in London, with heavy leather armchairs and a carpet of a pattern and colour ideal for concealing stains of spilled port. He had to wait alone for twenty minutes before the steward brought in a lady dressed in black and wearing a heavy veil. The veil did not prevent the lady from holding out her hand to be kissed before she sat down and the steward left.

'Monsieur Gautier,' she said, 'I am grateful to you for agreeing to meet me this afternoon.'

'Madame, if I can be of service . . .' Gautier left the sentence unfinished.

'I need advice and my friends assure me there is no person better qualified to give it.' She paused, no doubt to allow the importance of the compliment to be appreciated. Then she continued, 'I have recently, very recently, lost my husband in most distressing circumstances.'

'Would that have been in Dijon?'

'How very perspicacious of you.'

He could not see the expression on her face, but the tone of her comment suggested that she did not appreciate his attempt to make it easier for her to reach the point of what she wished to tell him.

'You met my husband, I believe.'

'I did once, very briefly, and I know the circumstances of his death.'

'I am told that quite soon I will have to give evidence before Judge Jolivet.'

'You will, and I trust it will not be too distressing for you.'

'That is not what is causing me concern. What I need from you is advice on what I should tell him.'

'Tell him the truth, Madame.'

'I will, of course, but as you must know, Inspector, truth comes in many forms.' Madame O'Flynn sighed and began lifting up her veil. 'You will not mind if I remove this emblem of mourning, will you? When people talk one should be able to look into their eyes.'

Gautier had to accept that for her age she was an exceptionally good-looking woman; typically French. No one could ever have taken her for American or even Dutch. He supposed she must be approaching fifty but she looked younger, with a skin free of wrinkles and a firm independent chin. If one were to find fault in her beauty, it would be for the discontent in her eyes, a look which had an air of permanence, the discontent of someone who felt life treated her unjustly.

'I will answer the judge's questions truthfully of course,' she said, 'but should I also volunteer any information?'

Gautier resisted a mischievous temptation to tell her that it would be safe to volunteer information provided it did not incriminate her. Instead he said, 'I am sure the judge would appreciate hearing anything you know which might help him achieve the objective of his examination.'

'Which is to establish who murdered my husband?'

'Exactly. In most cases the motive for murder is either greed or revenge. The judge will wish to know either who stood to gain from your husband's death, or who had a grudge against him.'

'You make it sound so simple. How can one be sure of who gains from Michael's death? One might say that financially I am the only one who benefits, for I inherit the château, the vineyard and all his property.'

'I am sure no one would suggest that you might have had him killed in order to inherit.'

'I would hope not! But there are others who will benefit in a different way.'

'Who, for example?'

'My two daughters, much though they loved Michael, will be glad to have their freedom.'

Gautier made no comment, for he sensed that Madame O'Flynn was ready to justify what she had said.

She looked at him for a moment and then continued almost defiantly, 'Michael had Victorian ideas on how to bring up his daughters; I suppose it was his Irish blood.'

Gautier might have pointed out that none of the Irish he had known would appreciate being associated, however remotely, with Queen Victoria.

She went on, 'My daughters are French, unmistakably so and yet he insisted on giving them Irish names; Bronagh and Cara. Can you imagine it? And he was reluctant to allow them to marry. He either believed that no man was good enough for them, or he suspected that any suitors might only be interested in getting their hands on his precious vineyard.' She sniffed and then added contemptuously, 'He seemed to forget that his Irish ancestor only acquired the vineyard by marrying into a French family.'

'Your daughters are still not too old to marry?'

'By no means! I will have them married off in no time.'

'And what will happen to the vineyard?'

She hesitated, as though uncertain of how much she should tell him.

'As yet I have not made up my mind. I may appoint a capable man to manage it, or I may sell it. That would allow me to give each of my daughters a generous dowry and still leave me enough to live in comfort.'

'At the Château Perdrix?'

'Probably not.' Again there was a hesitation. 'Inspector you can have no idea of how dreary life in the provinces can be; no theatres, no smart restaurants, no social life. I feel that perhaps I need a change. I might come and live in Paris for a time. For a widow, life in Burgundy would be stifling. Can you see that?'

'I can understand why you might feel that way,' Gautier replied diplomatically.

Madame O'Flynn was silent for a time. Then she seemed to come to a decision.

'Inspector there is one thing I must tell you. Indeed that was the main purpose of my coming to speak with you.'

'Madame?'

'You may have been wondering why it was that on the night he was murdered my husband was spending the night at a Dijon hotel. I can tell you it was not simply to avoid the inconvenience of returning home late at night. The truth is that earlier in the day Michael and I had quarrelled. Oh yes, we had quarrelled before – often. But this was more serious, the worst quarrel ever. I had told him that I was going to leave him.'

Gautier rode back to the Sûreté on a horse-drawn omnibus. His choice of transport was not made in deference to the Director General's determination to save money, but through nostalgia. Horse-drawn public vehicles were already being replaced by those powered by the internal combustion engine and although he could accept the need for progress, on a fine evening he knew he would enjoy a ride on the upper deck or *imperiale* of the old buses.

As he rode through Paris, he was speculating on the reasons why Madame O'Flynn had wished to meet him. The advice for which she seemed to be asking was of little moment and in any case she had given the impression of being a woman who would not take kindly to advice. She might possibly have been hoping that, after his meeting with Judge Jolivet, he would give her an insight into how the *instruction* would be conducted, but if so why? She had nothing to fear from any questions she might be asked.

When they had finished their discussion and she was about to leave he had asked, purely as a courtesy, whether he might go down with her to the carriage that was waiting outside for her and tell the coachman where she wished to be driven. She had replied sharply, 'He knows where to go!'. Gautier knew that the Prefect, like many men in Paris, kept a small apartment where he sometimes entertained his mistress of the moment. Was Madame O'Flynn on her way to the Prefect of Police's *garconnière* and had her meeting with Gautier been no more than a device to conceal her real reason for coming to Paris? By all accounts she and the Prefect had once been close friends and now her husband was dead. Gautier had always had the highest regard for the ability and integrity of the Prefect, but he found himself wondering what role he was playing in the Dijon affair.

Back in his office at Sûreté headquarters, he found two messages from Surat waiting on his desk. One told him that Surat had that afternoon visited the hotels to which Stephanie Winstock might have gone when she was looking for Lady Jane Shelford. At two of them no one remembered an American lady calling to ask whether an English milady was staying there. The concierge at the third one, the Hôtel Trumpington, did recollect an American calling and making enquiries about a Lady Shelford, but nothing more. Surat's message ended with a rather cryptic remark that he was not satisfied with what he had learnt at the hotels and that he planned to make further enquiries.

Surat's second message was that an American, a clergyman, had arrived at Sûreté headquarters, demanding to see Chief Inspector Gautier. The American who had given his name as Bishop James Arkwright, had been accompanied by an American lady and was clearly in a bad temper. In a most arrogant and high-handed manner he had insisted that he be taken to Inspector Gautier. Surat had told him that the Chief Inspector was not at Sûreté headquarters. The bishop had then announced that he would go immediately to see Paris's Chief of Police to complain about the way he had been treated. Eventually he had been partly pacified with a promise that Gautier would contact him at his hotel as soon as he returned to his office.

After reading the message Gautier decided that he would contact Bishop Arkwright, but not immediately. It was Saturday and he always made it a rule to clear his desk on Saturday evenings, so that there would be no outstanding problems for the duty inspector on Sunday or for himself on the following Monday. That evening what he needed to do was not arduous. A dozen or so reports lay in front of him and after reading them, he had either to decide what action should be taken, or endorse what was proposed. Even so it took time and by the time he was ready to leave for the Hôtel Cheltenham, it was after six o'clock.

He thought it easier to go and see the bishop in person rather than set up a meeting in his office. Confronting a man who believed he had a grievance was often a way of defusing his indignation and a visit to the Hôtel Cheltenham would also enable him to check on how Lady Jane was standing up to the shock of Stephanie Winstock's murder. He had some sympathy for what she must feel at the prospect of a further weekend alone in Paris.

When he reached the hotel, he was told by the concierge that Bishop Arkwright and Mrs Barclay were no longer there. They had left not long ago to catch a train for Dijon. Their rooms at the hotel was being kept for them, as they expected to return by not later than Monday evening. Gautier could guess what had happened. Judge Jolivet would be starting his *instruction* on Monday morning and the bishop would be among the first to be questioned. Whether he would be allowed to leave Dijon and return to Paris was a matter for the judge.

While he was talking to the concierge Gautier had been aware that a woman had arrived at the desk and was waiting impatiently. She would be in her early forties, he supposed, not fashionably dressed and almost certainly not French. Her eyes behind her spectacles were full of anxiety.

'Monsieur,' she said to the concierge as Gautier began to move away, 'would you be kind enough to have my luggage brought down from my room?'

'Certainly, Mademoiselle.'

'Quickly, if you please. I am pressed for time. Oh, and could you tell me how I can get to the Gare du Nord?' Her French was reasonable but awkwardly phrased; the stiff, formal French taught at a good English school.

'I can order a fiacre to take you there.'

The woman was carrying a small purse and she began peering into it, counting the coins. Gautier was not sure whether she was seeing if she had enough money for a fiacre, or whether she was looking for a tip to give the concierge. Whatever she found in her purse only seemed to sharpen her anxiety.

'As you will know, my employer will be settling the account for my stay at the hotel,' she said, 'so would you please have my luggage brought down?'

Gautier realized then that this must be Miss Sarah Boyle, the travelling companion of Lady Jane. Immediately he grew suspicious. Miss Boyle must be intending to catch the boat train from the Gare du Nord, which must mean she was returning to England. Could this be part of a plan for her and Lady Jane to leave Paris secretly?

'How long will it take me to reach the station in a fiacre?' she asked the concierge. 'On no account must I miss the train.'

Gautier stopped and turned to face her. 'Mademoiselle, can I be of assistance?'

Now it was Miss Boyle's turn to be suspicious.

'Who are you, Monsieur?'

'Chief Inspector Gautier. I am known to Lady Jane.'

Suspicion was replaced by relief. 'Oh yes. Lady Jane says you have been very kind to her.'

'Are you returning to England? Alone?'

'Yes. It is a matter of a family bereavement.' There were tears behind Miss Boyle's spectacles.

'In that case you must allow me to escort you to the railway station. You should not be travelling alone in Paris at this hour.'

Miss Boyle's protests were no more than a token as Gautier took charge of the arrangements for her departure. He was not sure why he was making the gesture; a feeling of guilt perhaps for his suspicions of her behaviour. In a matter of minutes they were together in a fiacre heading for the Gare du Nord. Her father, a clergyman in a country parish, was dying, she told him and Lady Jane had insisted that she should return home. She was plainly worried about the journey, for which she had tickets for the train and boat, but nothing more.

'Did you come to the hotel this evening to see Lady Jane?' she asked him.

'No, only to enquire after her. I came to see an American bishop, but he had left the hotel.'

'Bishop Arkwright? That dreadful man! Lady Jane and I have been trying to avoid meeting him.'

'Why do you dislike him? Has he been offensive to you?'

'Not me personally, but his behaviour has shocked many people, including my father.'

She told him the story. Her father, it seemed, had taken his degree at Cambridge as a member of a small college with ecclesiastical connections. Former members of the college were allowed from time to time to dine there, joining the dons on the top table. On one occasion not long previously Bishop Arkwright had also been taken to dine in hall as the guest of one of the fellows of the college. Half-way through the dinner, he had stood up, uninvited, and launched into a speech, attacking the college, its members and traditions.

'For serving wine?'

'How did you know? My father and everyone at the top table were appalled, not by what he said, which was offensive enough, but by his arrogance and impertinence.'

'What happened?'

Everyone at the top table had listened in silence, Miss Boyle said, but soon the undergraduates in the body of the hall grew restless. Someone began to heckle and presently booing began, reinforced by the undergraduates banging on the tables with their beer tankards. Finally Bishop Arkwright was forced to abandon what he was saying and sat down.

'It did not stop there,' Miss Boyle concluded. 'The Master and Fellows decided that the undergraduates had been guilty of an unforgivable display of discourtesy and the whole college was gated for a week.'

'Gated?'

'That means they were not allowed to leave the college in the evenings. So you see, Cambridge does not have happy memories of Bishop Arkwright.'

When they reached the Gare du Nord, Gautier took Miss Boyle to the office of the Chef de Gare, where he asked her to give him her tickets for the train and boat journeys. Leaving her outside the office he went inside, returning a few minutes later with new tickets which he gave her.

'Here you are,' he said. 'Now you have a first-class ticket on the train to Calais. When you board the steamer go to the office of the purser who has arranged a berth for you. You will be sharing a cabin with another lady, also as it happens, the daughter of a clergyman.'

Miss Boyle stared at him. 'But I cannot pay for all this!'

'There is no need for payment. The tickets come with the compliments of the French railways. They should help to make your-joumey a little more comfortable.'

Now there were real tears in Miss Boyle's eyes. Gautier knew they were not so much tears of gratitude, but of relief. Any woman of her age would have been dreading travelling alone at night by train and boat to England and he was surprised that Lady Jane had been willing to allow her to make such a journey. The boat-train was not due to leave for another hour, so they went to the station restaurant where the staff were persuaded, though with some reluctance, to make Miss Boyle a pot of tea. The French still did not understand the English passion for tea. Gautier thought that he had earned a coffee and a cognac for himself.

As they were sitting chatting, Miss Boyle suddenly said, 'You will look after Lady Jane when I am gone, will you not, Inspector? I know she is upset at having to stay on in Paris alone over the weekend.'

'Has she no friends here?'

'None to speak of. She and I came to Paris a few weeks ago, but that was her first visit since she was brought here as a girl by her parents years ago.'

'Do you know why she chose to stay at the Hôtel Cheltenham?'

Miss Boyle shrugged. 'I suspect that was just a whim. When we came here earlier this year we stayed at the Hôtel Trumpington, which was where Lady Jane had stayed with her parents years ago, but frankly we were disappointed with the standard of service it provided. Lady Jane may well have chosen the Hôtel Cheltenham only because Cheltenham was where she had been educated.'

9

As he sat in the barber's chair, Gautier reflected on how Sunday mornings had changed for him. Years previously when his wife Suzanne was alive and they were living together, he had looked forward to Sundays, to lying in bed and enjoying the silence, the absence of cries of street traders and of carriage wheels bumping across the cobbles outside their apartment. Then there would be a kind of family ritual, going to Mass, after which they would be taken to lunch by her father and mother, usually in a good bourgeois restaurant or in summer at a *guinguette* by the Seine; lunches marked by friendly banter and more than one bottle of good wine, with cognac and perhaps a cigar to follow.

After Suzanne had died family Sundays were over. From time to time he would spend the day with his current mistress and he had hoped that he might have spent this Sunday with Ingrid. Now Ingrid was in America and all he had left was the luxury of having his hair cut, his beard trimmed and hot towels round his face. The barber, an enterprising fellow who opened his shop on Sundays, drew most of his clientele from men arriving in Paris at the nearby Gare St Lazare. Because he seldom knew them well, he was taciturn, certainly not a conversationalist. That suited Gautier because Sunday was one of the times during the week when he could think undisturbed.

Looking back over the events of the past few days, he was glad that he had been able to smooth her journey home for Miss Sarah Boyle. The role of travelling companion to a wealthy woman was not one which he really understood, for he had met only one before Miss Boyle. He supposed there might be certain advantages for the companion, allowing her to travel in countries other than her own and enjoying opportunities to visit museums, art galleries and spectacles which otherwise would not be open to her. To counter this there was an element of subservience which he found distasteful.

In the case of Miss Boyle, he found it disturbing that Lady Jane should have allowed her companion, a middle-aged woman, unequipped apart from her slender knowledge of French, to embark on an overnight journey travelling alone in conditions of minimum comfort. If he were to have an opportunity he might speak to Lady Jane about it, even though any reproaches he might make were unlikely to have any effect on her.

When the hairdresser had finished with him, he decided it would do no harm to look in at his office in Quai des Orfèvres. On a Sunday there would probably be nothing which merited his attention, but he was sure he could find something in the office to occupy the empty hours before he took his lunch in some nearby café. As the day was fine, he walked past the Madeleine and across the Jardin des Tuileries, towards the Seine. Overlooking the river several *bouquinistes* had set out their stalls of second-hand books, not as many as one would find on a weekday, but they were doing some trade among passers-by who, like him, were filling in time, strolling in the sunshine.

He had just reached the point where he should cross the road and make his way to the entrance of Sûreté headquarters when he noticed a man leaning over the parapet and staring into the river. Something about the man's figure and posture looked familiar, but he needed a second or two to realize that it was Raymond

Ferry, the official from the American Embassy. Ferry must have become aware of his presence for he looked round.

'Inspector Gautier!'

They shook hands. 'What are you doing in this part of Paris, Monsieur Ferry?'

'To tell you the truth I am not entirely sure myself. I came here to find out whether by any chance you were in your office today.'

'And you were told that I was not?'

'Yes, but they said you often looked in at about this time on a Sunday. So I decided to wait, but then I began to wonder whether I should be coming to see you at all.'

'You have something to tell me?'

Ferry looked embarrassed. 'Put it this way. I am not sure whether I should tell you, not officially at least.'

'Then why not tell me anyway and if I agree that it is not something you should have told me, I will forget it. Shall we go in to my office?'

'Could we not talk here?'

'Certainly. That will make our conversation absolutely unofficial.'

Ferry smiled, but it was obvious that he was still uncomfortable. 'You have been so fair in your treatment of Miss Pauline Fenn, too fair perhaps, that I feel that you should know what I am going to tell you. One might also say that it is my duty to do what I can to assist the police in their investigation into the murder of Stephanie Winstock. After all she too was an American citizen.'

Gautier waited. He had begun to sense what Ferry might be going to tell him, but it was better that the man should say it in his own time and in his own way.

After a moment more of hesitation Ferry continued, 'You have of course seen Miss Fenn's account of how she and Miss Winstock spent their first days in Paris.'

'I have, yes.'

'I regret to say, Inspector, that a good deal of that account was false. Miss Fenn lied.'

'How do you know that?'

'She told my wife so. In the short time that she has been staying in our home Miss Fenn has struck up a rapport with my wife. She has told her in some detail of her relationship with her employer. And she has admitted that much of the statement she made was untrue.'

'What in particular?'

'Everything she said concerning their attempt to find out where Lady Jane was staying was false. It all seems to have been the consequence of a deception which she began back in America.'

Pauline Fenn, Ferry told Gautier, had been responsible for making the travel and hotel arrangements for their visit to France. Miss Winstock had wished to stay in the Hôtel Trumpington, but Pauline was determined that they should not stay there. Without even approaching the hotel, she had told Miss Winstock that it had no rooms available for the period of their visit and instead had booked them in at the Pension Beau Séjour where eventually Winstock was murdered.

'Why did Miss Fenn object to the Hôtel Trumpington?' Gautier asked.

'As far as I can tell simply because she believed Lady Jane Shelford might be staying there. Apparently she had stayed there during her last visit to Paris.'

'Could it have been that Fenn did not want the two women to stay in the same hotel while they were in Paris?'

The question seemed to make Ferry uncomfortable. 'Very possibly. It is also untrue that they were pleased with the Pension Beau Séjour into which she had booked them. Miss Winstock made it clear that she was far from satisfied.'

'Perhaps she objected to the fact that they had been given just the one room to share.'

'That may be so. Miss Fenn was told to check with the Hôtel Trumpington to find out if it had any free rooms now, failing which she was to find them another hotel.'

'Had she?'

Not as far as I know. What I do know is that everything she said about Miss Winstock visiting hotels to find out where Lady Jane was, was so untrue. At some point Miss Winstock telephoned the Hôtel Cheltenham and learnt that Lady Jane was staying there. She went to see her as soon as she was free after her meeting.'

'You say she told your wife all this?'

'Yes. I do not know why. Perhaps she was trying to impress my wife by showing her how clever she is, how skilful she had been in manipulating Miss Winstock.' Ferry paused and then added lamely, 'Miss Fenn appears to have a very compelling way with other women.'

Alone in his office, Gautier thought about what Ferry had told him. The man had done what he obviously believed to be his duty, even though the telling had made him feel uncomfortable. Could it be that he was regretting taking Pauline Fenn into his home and might that be because of the relationship which was developing between her and his wife? Although Gautier recognized that the sympathy he had felt for Pauline when she was put in prison was probably misplaced, there seemed to be nothing in what Ferry had told him to suggest that she might have been responsible for the death of Stephanie Winstock. And yet he could not help feeling that a better understanding of the relationship between the three women, Winstock, Fenn and Lady Jane Shelford, might help to point him towards solving the murder.

He remembered that Lady Jane was still in Paris and, on her

own admission, hating the prospect of spending a Sunday alone in the city. That gave him an idea. He saw that it would soon be midday and there was every chance that she would in due course be lunching at her hotel, very probably in her suite. Twenty minutes of conversation with her before then might give him answers to some of the questions which were puzzling him. The correct course would be for him to send a message, asking whether she would agree to see him, but he rejected the thought. She would find it more difficult to refuse to see him if he presented himself at the hotel.

When he reached the Cheltenham, he found that the hotel was unusually quiet, the lobby almost empty. As the weather was fine, any visitors who might be staying there would be out, gazing at the sights which Paris had to offer. He told the concierge that he would like to be taken up by a page to Lady Jane's suite. If the man was surprised, he concealed it and replied that he would take the inspector up himself, assuming that Gautier had come on police business. He may have even wondered whether Lady Jane was to be arrested. Such things were not unknown, even at a hotel with the Cheltenham's exclusive reputation.

When they reached the suite, the concierge knocked on the outer door, waited until he heard Lady Jane's voice and then went in, leaving Gautier in the corridor outside. A moment or two later he returned.

'Her ladyship has agreed to see you,' he said, 'but perhaps you would wait in the drawing-room until she has had time to get ready.'

Gautier suppressed a smile. On two of his previous visits Lady Jane had kept him waiting and on the last occasion Pierre Desportes had teased him, suggesting that she might be beautifying herself for him. The concierge left and he waited alone in the drawing-room. When Lady Jane arrived, she did not seem to have spent too much trouble over her appearance. Gautier wondered, not for the first time, why it was that English women were either apathetic about what they wore, or had no sense of style.

'I must apologize for disturbing you, Madame,' he said.

'No need for apologies, Inspector, but I was just about to go out,' Lady Jane replied and then she added, 'I have decided I cannot just stay here on my own, moping.'

'If I may ask where were you going, Madame?'

'Just for a stroll. They tell me many French ladies of good standing take a stroll in the mornings and I certainly need the exercise.'

Gautier could detect a change in her manner since they had last met. Perhaps he had misjudged her and she was more resolute than he had supposed, when he had learnt how easily she had succumbed to the plausible cajolery of a confidence trickster. He was surprised even so that she seemed to be recovering from the grief she had shown at the death of Stephanie Winstock.

'Where were you planning to lunch?' he asked her.

'Here in the hotel, where else?'

'May I make a suggestion, Madame? It is growing late. Would you allow me to take you to lunch first and afterwards you could have your stroll?'

She did not seem surprised by his suggestion. She hesitated, but not for too long.

'Thank you. That is most kind of you. I accept, but only provided you do not take me to anywhere expensive. First you must allow me to fetch a hat.'

As they were walking downstairs to the ground floor Gautier said, 'If you agree we can go to a good bourgeois restaurant which I know and which caters for families. The family lunch is an institution in France. All the members of the family lunch in a restaurant together; grandparents, aunts and uncles, cousins, even small children. They wear their best clothes and behave with serious decorum. Is it the same in England?'

'Not really. In England on Sundays a family will lunch together but at home and without ceremony.'

They were driven in a fiacre to a restaurant in a small street not far from Place d'Iéna; one of the restaurants to which he and his wife had sometimes been taken by her parents. He had not eaten there for some years but he remembered that though the place was unpretentious, the food had always been good. They were given a table for two and as they ordered they saw the other larger tables filling up with families. At every table wine was being poured for the children as well as adults, a glass for each of the older children and half a glass for the youngest.

'Look! Children who cannot be older than eight are being given wine!' Lady Jane exclaimed.

'Just half a glass topped up with water,' Gautier replied. 'That is the French way. Learning how to drink is part of our education.'

'Bishop Arkwright would have a brainstorm if he were here.'

'You know the bishop then?'

'I met him just once. An odious man!'

'Where was that? Here in France?'

'No, in London. He and Steve were both speaking at a conference organized by an English temperance group. I went there at the end simply to collect Steve and take her back to my home.'

'Mademoiselle Winstock stayed with you in England then?'

'Often. We used to meet every year for two or three weeks, always in England. This was to be the first time we met in Europe. Steve was coming to Paris to organize a French branch of her association and would not be able to spare the time to visit England as well. So we agreed to meet in Paris and have our holiday here after the meetings were over.'

'With Pauline Fenn?'

'Certainly not! She was to return to the States immediately after the meetings.'

Gautier had been wondering whether over lunch Lady Jane might be willing to talk about Stephanie Winstock. Now she had begun to do so without any prompting and she did not seem to find the subject of their friendship too painful to recount. She told him more about Stephanie Winstock's annual visits to England.

'That was her holiday, the only holiday she ever took. We would go for long walks in the country and talk for hours about art, books, history, philosophy; everything except temperance. That was taboo.'

Gautier smiled as he pointed at the glass of wine in front of her. 'But not about wine, I presume?'

'Steve did not drink. It was against her principles, but she had no objection to my taking a glass of wine. She was very tolerant, you know.' Gautier did not like to point out that most supporters of temperance, Stephanie Winstock included, were renowned for their bigotry. Lady Jane continued, 'They were wonderful days. Idyllic was how Steve used to describe them. We were so happy together until that girl came along.'

'Mademoiselle Fenn?'

'Yes. The Women's Christian Temperance Association made Steve take her on as her secretary. They said Steve was working too hard and needed help which was true, but Pauline was a bad choice. From the day she was appointed she seemed determined to drive a wedge between us; would never leave us alone together. Why was that, do you think?'

'She appears to have a very jealous disposition.'

'Let us not talk about her. It makes me so cross!'

Lady Jane gave a grimace of disgust. She had shown little distress as she talked of a woman whom she had clearly loved and who had been murdered in a particularly brutal way, and now she was ready to drop the subject and talk of something else. Could this be just the sang-froid of the English or was her manner just a façade, concealing a turmoil of grief underneath? During the rest of their lunch they talked of other things. Gautier formed the impression that she was a highly educated and cultured woman and that for most of the time she kept any susceptible emotions which she might have well under control.

He was surprised to learn that she was knowledgeable about wine. He had ordered a bottle of red wine for them and she sipped from her glass with obvious pleasure. When he told her it was from Burgundy she seemed surprised. At home most people who cared for wine, she told him, preferred wines from Bordeaux. Her father had been a connoisseur and had brought his children up to recognize and appreciate its fine qualities.

When they had finished lunch and were about to leave the restaurant, she asked him: 'Well, where do you suggest that we take our stroll?'

'Must it be a stroll? Have you ever been on the Seine? I always feel that from the river one sees the best of Paris.'

'All right, if that is what you recommend. There would be no chance of *mal-de-mer* I hope.'

She accepted his reassurance on the subject of sea-sickness and they walked down to a pier on the Seine, from where they could board a *bateau mouche*. As the afternoon was fine, the boat was almost full and there were crowds of people on both banks of the Seine as well as on the bridges, some strolling, some leaning on the parapets over the water. The boat sailed at a leisurely speed towards Nôtre Dame and Gautier pointed out some of the landmarks which were making Paris an attraction to foreign visitors. The excursion was a popular one, especially on Sundays, but Lady

Jane did not seem to mind the noise and exuberance of the other passengers.

When they were rounding the Ile de la Cité she said, 'By the way, do you have any news of that scoundrel who swindled me out of my money?'

'I regret to say no, but our enquiries are continuing. I am certain we will track him down eventually. There can be few confidence tricksters operating at that level of society.'

'Steve might have been able to give me his real name.'

'Why? How was Mademoiselle Winstock involved?'

'An American friend of hers was also a victim of a swindler. At least the man who took her money used the same ruse and claimed that he had discovered gold in Algeria. He used a different name; Paul Delarue, but it must have been the same man. She too met him at a reception given by the Comtesse de Fleury.'

Lady Jane told Gautier that Stephanie Winstock's friend, a Mrs Harrington of New York, was a wealthy supporter of the temperance cause. She was also a very determined lady who resented parting with several thousands of dollars and wanted to make the swindler pay for his insolence. When she realized that she had been duped, she had hired Wilmingtons, an American detective agency, to find him. Gautier knew that Wilmington's was one of the largest detective agencies in the United States and that it also had branches in Europe.

'This Mrs Harrington must have been swindled of a great deal of money, to have gone to such trouble.'

'Not much more than me, I understand, but she is not a lady who likes to look foolish. In England we would describe her as a bad loser. Apparently Wilmingtons traced the man who took her money, but she will not be able to get it back.'

'Why not?'

'Wilmingtons say it would be pointless to sue him. It seems she handed her money over in such a way that he could claim it was an unsolicited gift. So he cannot be said to have done anything illegal. Mrs Harrington is furious.'

'But she knows the swindler's name?'

'Wilmingtons do; his real name, his address, everything. She wrote to them demanding to be told, but the information had not arrived when Steve left for Paris. Steve planned to visit the detective agency as soon as she had time, find out the swindler's name and pass it on to Mrs Harrington.'

'And to you?'

She shrugged. 'I would be interested to know it, but I have already written off the money I gave Monsieur Desfontaines as the price of a foolish indiscretion.'

10

Next morning Gautier went with Courtrand to the Palais de Justice for a meeting with Judge Loubet, who had been appointed *juge d'instruction* for the murder of Stephanie Winstock. In the normal way the judge, as soon as he was appointed, would hold a preliminary meeting with the police officer in charge, so that he could be brought up to date with progress in the investigation and begin planning how he should conduct the *instruction*. There was no reason why the Director General of the Sûreté should be present at the meeting and Courtrand had only gone because the investigation was into the death of an American citizen. Having for some time assiduously watched over the interests of English visitors in Paris, he now wished to show that he was equally solicitous for Americans.

'Our relations with America,' he told Judge Loubet, 'will be enhanced if we apprehend the murderer of this lady as soon as possible.'

'Provided of course that it does not happen to be another American,' the judge replied gently.

Judge Loubet was one of the examining magistrates whom Gautier had always respected. Fair and patient, he would not allow himself to be distracted from his pursuit of the truth by irrelevancies which witnesses at an *instruction* frequently introduced, either through delusions of self-importance or deliberately to conceal the truth.

'Well, Gautier,' he said after brushing aside Courtrand's comment. 'What progress have you made in this affair?'

'I regret to say very little, Monsieur le Juge. At first sight it would appear to be a murder without a motive.'

'They are rare, are they not?'

'Very rare fortunately, for they are the most intractable.'

Gautier explained that the murder of Winstock did not appear to have been for theft or gain and there had been no sign of sexual assault. As far as the police knew the victim did not have any enemies in France at least, or at the most only one. Enquiries had shown that on the evening of the murder, Bishop Arkwright had been attending a meeting of French Methodists, at which he had spoken on the evils of intemperance.

'I was not aware that there was a Methodist church in France,' Loubet said.

'There is and it is surprisingly active. At least sixty people could testify that on the evening of the murder they were obliged to endure a homily from the bishop which lasted for more than two hours.'

'I had heard,' Loubet remarked, 'that another American lady, Mademoiselle Winstock's secretary, had been placed under arrest.'

'She was for a time and later released into the custody of the American Embassy.'

'You had a good reason for that I am sure.'

Gautier told the judge why he had allowed the release from prison of Pauline Fenn. Although, after hearing what she had told Madame Ferry, he no longer felt any pity for Fenn, he did not believe that she could have killed Winstock. She had behaved irrationally, but that might well have been because she was an unstable personality, engulfed in an infatuation she could no longer control and driven by jealousy which went beyond reason.

'In that case you were right to release the woman,' Courtrand said pompously. Then he added, 'Now gentlemen I must leave you. I am expecting a visitor; the Chief of Police from Madrid. He wishes to model his force on mine.'

Although he did not say as much, one had the feeling that Judge Loubet was not sorry to see Courtrand leave. Nor was Gautier. The man had not contributed anything to their discussion and it seemed unlikely that he would. After he had left Loubet and Gautier began to discuss the timing of the instruction or judicial examination.

'In view of the slow progress that has so far been made in your investigations,' Loubet said, 'do you think we should postpone starting it?'

'Not necessarily. There can be advantages in starting early. Witnesses who prevaricate when questioned by the police are sometimes frightened into telling the truth when faced with an official enquiry.'

Loubet laughed. 'In that case I must remember to adopt a more aggressive attitude. So you would have no objections if we were to start tomorrow?'

'Why not? Most of the witnesses you might wish to call have been alerted already. If we do start the hearing tomorrow, may I suggest that a witness to be called early should be the English woman, Lady Jane Shelford. She was an intimate friend of Winstock and, it seems, the last person to have spent any time with her before her death.'

'Then she appears to be a logical choice.'

In the next hour the judge and Gautier discussed the timing of the judicial examination and the choice of witnesses. They both recognized that, since the investigation of the crime was at an early stage, any arrangements they might make must be provisional. Under French law the examination was a vital stage in the process by which criminals could be brought to justice. Its purpose was to assemble and scrutinize all the evidence relating to a crime and then to pass it to the *Chambre des Mises en Accusations*, a panel of judges which would decide whether a prosecution should be made.

Other countries had different systems and that of France was sometimes criticized as being too cumbersome and bureaucratic. Gautier did not agree. In France the decision on whether or not a criminal prosecution should be started was made by experts, people trained in the law. In England, on the other hand, magistrates were very often amateurs, recruited from the well-to-do middle classes, with no legal training and in many cases. they were middle-aged ladies with no qualifications at all, except time to spare and a willingness to meddle in the affairs of others.

Gautier gave the judge a brief account of his investigations into the death of Stephanie Winstock and promised to write a report summarizing everything that had happened which he would send to the Palais de Justice that afternoon. He also warned Loubet that Pauline Fenn had already in effect changed the evidence she had given and might well do so again. When he returned to his office at Sûreté headquarters he found Surat waiting for him.

'I have to tell you that I have made further enquiries regarding the Hotel Trumpington, Patron,' Surat told him.

'When did you do that; not on Sunday surely?'

'No, on Saturday evening.'

Gautier guessed then what Surat must have done. In a criminal investigation when any questions he had asked at a hotel or private home did not produce a positive response, he would return to the district on his own in the evening and try to mix with the staff during their leisure hours. Sometimes he would simply listen to what they were saying to each other. At other times he would join their conversations which, as a sociable and unassuming fellow, was not difficult for him. The gossip of servants had often given him a rewarding insight into matters which would not be discussed in working hours.

'You should have been at home with your family,' Gautier reproved him.

Surat took no notice of the reproach. 'What I had been told when I visited the hotel officially was not the whole truth. It is true that an American lady visited the hotel on the day in question, but her visit was not without incident.'

'What happened?'

The American lady, Surat told him, had caused trouble. Her attitude had been rude and belligerent. She had sent for the manager and complained that she had been told there were no rooms available at the hotel, which was untrue. Now she demanded that as recompense she and her companion should be given rooms without charge. She threatened to tell the newspapers how badly she had been treated.

'That is a device some visitors use to get cheap accommodation.'

'I do not believe it was in this instance. She appears to have gone to the hotel with the intention of making trouble. The manager tried to pacify her as tactfully as he could, but she would not listen and a noisy row developed. Other guests, mainly French people, witnessed it and some of them laughed, but it was embarrassing. I do not believe the lady would be welcome there if she were to visit the hotel again.'

'When did all this incident take place?'

'In the afternoon.'

'Did you find out the woman's name?'

'Oh, yes. She made no secret of it. She was a Mademoiselle Stephanie Winstock.'

As he walked along Boulevard St Germain on his way to the Café Corneille, Gautier was thinking of what Surat had told him. It was clear now that not only had Pauline Fenn's account of how she and her employer had spent their first days in Paris been untrue, but that she had lied to Madame Ferry as well. He felt that he must find out the truth as soon as possible and certainly before Judge Loubet began his judicial examination. So before leaving his office, he had told Surat to go to the American Embassy and find out the names of the three women who were forming the French branch of the American Women's Temperance Association. By contacting one or all of the women they might be able to learn more of what Winstock had done during the first days after her arrival in France.

When he was approaching the café, a fiacre drew up in front of it. Duthrey got out and Gautier could tell from his manner and the drooping of his shoulders that his friend was upset. They shook hands but Duthrey did not speak as they made their way to the table where they always sat. None of the rest of their group had yet arrived.

'Do I get the impression, old friend,' Gautier said cheerfully, 'that the day is not going well for you?'

'There is nothing wrong with the day, or with me for that matter. I have had news from Dijon which is upsetting, nothing more.'

'Not bad news of Michael O'Flynn's family I trust?'

Duthrey did not answer until they were seated and had ordered their apéritifs. Then he said, 'The *Confrérie des Chevaliers du Tastevin* is to be disbanded.'

'Disbanded? Surely not?'

'Perhaps disbanded may not be the right word. The other officers of the *Confrérie* have decided to postpone holding any further *intronisations*.'

'For how long?'

'Indefinitely. O'Flynn was the moving force behind the whole idea and he carried the others with him. Now no one is prepared to take the lead, or to put up the finance required. Some are saying that forming a *Confrérie* was premature, that we should wait until wines from Burgundy are better established in world markets.'

Gautier remembered Pascal, who had been sitting next to him at the inaugural meeting of the *Confrérie* suggesting that many in the wine business held similar views. He wondered what he could say to console Duthrey, but before he had thought of anything he saw Froissart and the judge arriving.

'I would prefer it if you did not mention what I have told you to our other friends,' Duthrey said quickly. 'I would not like them to feel embarrassed.'

One could understand Duthrey's disappointment. His election as a Chevalier of the *Confrérie* had been a matter for pride, the first honour to be conferred on him and now he must feel that it had been snatched away from him. As it happened their friends at the café were not likely to discuss his honour that day, for their attention was soon focused on another more topical subject. The deputy for Seine-et-Marne had come there straight from a meeting of deputies which had been addressed that morning by the Prefect of Police.

The Prefect was a powerful figure in the life of Paris, in a position to promulgate regulations or decrees which could affect the social life of the city. Not many years previously his predecessor had announced that women would not be allowed to wear men's clothes in public. His action had caused controversy, for while the great majority of men had supported it, the growing number of liberal, emancipated young women had been outraged by this restriction on their liberty. It had become a challenge for many of them and they would go out wearing men's dress concealed beneath long cloaks.

The present Prefect had so far taken a more conservative line but now, according to the deputy, that was about to change. He had told the meeting that morning that he intended to revoke the existing restrictions and replace them with regulations which would not discriminate between the sexes and would treat everyone equally. This would bring many advantages to all ranks of society. For example, he had said, because of the changes he planned, married women would have greater rights, and divorce, which had been virtually restricted to the wealthy, would be easier for everyone.

Duthrey who believed passionately in the sanctity of marriage, was indignant when he heard the news.

'This will strike at the very basis of family life,' he said. 'Society as we know it will be destroyed.'

The young lawyer, who had arrived while the deputy was giving the news and who was acknowledged to be an expert on divorce, took a different view.

'Not at all. We are living in a modern world. It is intolerable that people who find they are incompatible should be forced to live together.'

'The only people who will gain,' Froissart remarked, 'are the lawyers.'

The argument continued but without becoming acrimonious. The habitués of the Café Corneille could hold sharply polarized views, but never allowed themselves to quarrel. As he listened to them, Gautier wondered whether the action of the Prefect might have been influenced by personal considerations. Madame

O'Flynn had said that she had intended to leave her husband and in view of the Prefect's obvious interest in the lady, was it possible that one of his motives for the changes he planned had been to make life easier for her?

The discussion at the café that day soon veered into other issues and Gautier thought no more about the Prefect until he and Duthrey had left together and were looking for a fiacre to take Duthrey home to his lunch. Then it was Duthrey who raised the subject.

'I had a letter from a friend in the wine trade in Beaune this morning,' he said, 'which leads me to wonder whether the Prefect is becoming too closely involved in what is happening there.'

'What did your friend say?'

'Simply that people there are beginning to question his interference in what they see as a domestic matter,' Duthrey replied. Then he added petulantly, 'It will only end by distracting attention from the more important issue of the future of the *Confrérie des Chevaliers du Tastevin*.'

After lunching at the café in Place Dauphine, Gautier returned to his office in the Sûreté headquarters where he found two messages waiting for him. One was from Surat. He had been to the American Embassy and found out the names of the three women whom Stephanie Winstock and Pauline had met on their second day in Paris. Apparently only one of the women lived in Paris, the other two having come in from the provinces for the meeting. The woman who lived in Paris was a Madame Pitot, the wife of a baker who had a shop in the 11th arrondissement. The second message was from the office of the Prefect of Police. The Prefect would be obliged if Chief Inspector Gautier would call at his office that afternoon.

With two options facing him, Gautier decided that he would go and question Madame Pitot. The baker's shop would certainly be open in the afternoon, while the Prefect might well be late in returning after lunching at his club. So he and Surat set out for the 11th arrondissement in one of the new motor omnibuses. The journey would have been quicker by Métro, but Surat was not yet prepared to face the dangers of subterranean travel.

Monsieur Pitot's shop was a thriving establishment with the baker himself serving and no fewer than three assistants. Madame Pitot, a formidable woman in a black dress, was seated behind the cashier's desk taking the customers' money. When Gautier introduced himself she left the desk and led him and Surat through the back of the shop and upstairs to the apartment where she and her husband lived. One could tell from the style of the apartment, with its heavy wooden furnishings and abundance of red plush, that the baker must be a man of some standing in the locality.

When all three of them were seated, she asked Gautier, 'You will take a glass, will you not, Inspector?' She pointed to a decanter of wine which stood on a table by the window. Although he was surprised by the invitation, Gautier knew that it would be bad manners to refuse. His surprise may have shown for Madame Pitot said, 'I can see that you know that I am involved in the temperance movement.'

'I heard as much, yes.'

'Allow me to explain. I embraced temperance not so much for myself as for my husband. Giving up drink has been the saving of him, of our business, and probably of his life.'

As Gautier and Surat sipped the glasses of very sweet red wine which she poured them, Madame Pitot explained that her husband had been a hopeless drunkard and their business on the verge of bankruptcy. By persuading him to stop drinking she had transformed his life. By saying that he had been converted to temperance he had avoided the shame of admitting that he could not control his drinking.

'Now neither of us drinks, Monsieur Gautier, but we would not deprive our friends of wine when they are in our home.'

Gautier could understand the rather convoluted logic which had guided Madame Pitot's actions. As a Frenchwoman, even though she was not against drink, she would also through a sense of duty feel obliged to give the temperance movement, which had saved her husband, her moral support.

'We are here, Madame, because we are investigating the death of Mademoiselle Stephanie Winstock,' he said.

'I guessed as much. Dreadful, was it not, unbelievable! Who could possibly have wished to murder her?'

'That is our principal difficulty; to find anyone with a reason for killing the lady. You were with her on the morning of her death, were you not?'

'Yes. We had a meeting with two other ladies and her secretary to discuss arrangements for the formation of a French branch of her movement.'

'How long did the meeting last? All day?'

'Not exactly. We continued our discussions over lunch. You see I invited Steve and the other two ladies to lunch. Nothing too grand you understand. We lunched in a modest restaurant not far from here where I am known.'

'The five of you?'

'No. My invitation did not include her secretary.' Madame Pitot looked at Gautier. With a less forthright woman one might have sensed that what she had to say embarrassed her. 'To be frank, Inspector, we none of us liked Pauline Fenn. She took too much on herself at the meeting, constantly interrupting our discussions and telling us what we should do. So I made a point in not inviting her to lunch. I do not think she was too pleased.'

'And how long did lunch last?'

'Well into the afternoon. Then Steve made a telephone call and learned that a good friend of hers was staying at the Hôtel Cheltenham. We left the restaurant and found her a fiacre to take her to the hotel.'

After leaving the baker's shop, Gautier and Surat separated, Gautier heading for the Prefect's office, while Surat went to the Hôtel Trumpington. What Madame Pitot had told them made it clear that Steve Winstock could not have been at the hotel during the afternoon before her murder. Surat's information had been based purely on gossip, on what he had heard from the hotel servants. Now Gautier told him to check the facts of what really had happened that afternoon, by questioning the staff at whatever level of seniority proved necessary. This was a major police investigation and he was not to allow himself to be put off with half-truths and evasions, however damaging the facts might be to the hotel's reputation.

Gautier went to the offices of the Prefect of Police where he found out that he had been right in making the visit to the baker's shop his first priority, for the Prefect had still not returned from his lunch. He did not have long to wait and when the Prefect did appear, he seemed to have forgotten having sent for Gautier. Then he remembered.

'Ah Gautier, come into my office. There have been developments in Dijon which concern you.' They went into his office and when they were alone, the Prefect continued, 'Judge Jolivet has begun his examination.'

'Has he questioned Madame O'Flynn yet, Monsieur?'

The Prefect looked at him sharply. 'Not as yet. There are other witnesses with more relevant experience to be examined first.'

'Bishop Arkwright for example.'

'Precisely. I spoke to the judge just after he had finished his morning session and I understand that the exact role which the bishop played in the events of that night is coming under scrutiny. It would seem that he has been less than honest in the account he gave of his movements.'

Gautier said nothing. There was more to come, he was sure of that. The Prefect made a great show of reading some messages which had arrived for him during lunch and which lay on his desk. Then he said, 'We do not know when Madame O'Flynn will be required to give evidence, but I want you to be ready to travel down to Dijon at a moment's notice to support her.'

'As a kind of prisoner's friend?'

The jocular question was likely to irritate the Prefect, but it did not needle him as much as one might have expected.

'Don't be absurd! Joséphine is not on trial! She may not even be called, but if she is it will be a painful experience. I want you to be there to guide and advise her. The focus of the examination has shifted on to your friend the bishop.'

Gautier refrained from pointing out that he had met Bishop Arkwright only once and then in circumstances not likely to encourage friendship. They talked for a little longer and the Prefect promised that he would telephone Gautier as soon as he knew that he was required in Dijon. On his way back to Sûreté headquarters, Gautier reflected that the murder of O'Flynn appeared to be affecting the very good relationship which he had always enjoyed with the Prefect. He also realized that his investigation of Stephanie Winstock's murder appeared to be becoming entangled with events in Dijon in a way that he had not expected.

Back at the Sûreté he found waiting for him a notice from Judge Loubet's office, which gave details of the preliminary arrangements for the instruction the following morning. The only witnesses to be called on the first day were those involved in the discovery of Stephanie Winstock's body, the proprietor of the Pension Beau Séjour, his wife, the guest who had first seen the body and the first policeman to arrive at the scene. That was to be expected and was correct procedure, but Gautier had been hoping that the proceedings could have been extended to include Lady Jane Shelford.

Once again he felt guilty, for he may have given Lady Jane the impression that she would be required to appear at the judicial examination on the first day, after which she would be free to leave France. Now she must stay on for at least one more day. This would distress her for she had made it clear that she dreaded having to stay on in Paris alone after the death of her friend. He supposed ways might be found to make her stay less harrowing.

Then he had an idea. The Gambon family's wine tasting was due to be held at six o'clock the following evening and Gautier had been invited to take a guest with him. There was no reason why Lady Jane should not be that guest, for she had shown that she was interested in wine. Accompanying Gautier to the tasting would occupy at least part of her day and give her something to which she could look forward while she waited to be called to Judge Loubet's instruction. He knew that he should ask her before naming her as his guest, but time was getting short and the invitation had asked that the names of guests should be submitted to the organizers of the event in advance. So he decided that he would telephone the Salle Delacroix at once and give Lady Jane Shelford's name. If when he invited her she declined to go, no great harm would have been done.

11

The first day of Judge Loubet's instruction was not expected to produce any new information relevant to the murder of Stephanie Winstock, for the witnesses examined were mainly from the pension where the dead woman's body had been found. The questions they were asked were based on the statements they had made to the police soon after the murder. In most cases they had nothing to add to what they had then said, although one or two of them, carried away by the importance of the occasion, could not resist the temptation to elaborate on their statements, trying to give the impression that they knew more than they had admitted. Judge Loubet listened to them patiently, too patiently Gautier was inclined to think, for he was soon finding the day becoming tedious.

Any vague hope he had held that during the examination more information about the mysterious Robinet would come to light was disappointed. None of the other guests at the pension appear to have spoken to the man, nor could they even give a description of him. One fact which did emerge was that he had not occupied the room next to that of the two Americans, as Gautier had assumed he might have done. In fact he had been lodged in a room on the second floor of the pension. Once he knew this, Gautier tried to reconstruct what must have happened. Since there had been no evidence of robbery or sexual assault, one might conclude that the murder had been planned or at least premeditated. Stephanie Winstock had been the target and the murderer had waited for her, stabbed her with a dagger he had brought with him and then used the empty room next door to conceal the weapon. If it had been Robinet and he had gone to the pension simply to carry out the murder, then an answer was needed to one more question.

In the French manner, the *instruction* was halted for two hours soon after midday to give everyone present an opportunity to have a worthwhile lunch. When they were breaking up Gautier had a word with Judge Loubet.

'It might be helpful to the investigation if we were to know at what time this man Robinet arrived at the pension,' he said.

'Do you suspect that he may have been involved in the murder?'

'Possibly, Monsieur le Juge, but that is largely because we have no other suspects.'

'I will ask the owner of the pension that question this afternoon. He must keep some record of the guests as they arrive.' Loubet looked at Gautier and smiled. 'We have made a good team over the last few years, Gautier, and I am confident that together we will solve this murder. If you wish to absent yourself from any session of my examination to pursue your enquiries in your own unconventional way, you have my permission to do so. I will see that a transcript of each day's proceedings will be on your desk first thing the following morning.'

That morning before leaving his office, Gautier had written a note to Lady Jane, inviting her to attend the wine tasting at the Salle Delacroix that evening as his guest. In the note he apologized for the lateness of the invitation and said he would explain the circumstances when they met. He had sent the note by hand to her hotel. Now during the lunch break when he returned to Sûreté headquarters, he found her reply waiting for him.

Monsieur,
I am conscious of the honour you have done me by your invitation, but regret that I cannot possibly accept. Indeed I have to say that I was surprised you could have imagined that I would welcome any social invitation so soon after the tragic demise of an intimate and much loved friend.

Lady Jane Shelford.

The manner and tone of Lady Jane's response would no doubt have offended most men, but Gautier only smiled and told himself that perhaps he had deserved the rebuke for his presumption. In any case the incident had provided him with a useful lesson in the ways of the English nobility.

He had just finished reading the note when Surat came into his office to report on what he had learned that morning at the Hôtel Trumpington. The manager of the hotel had under pressure admitted that what Surat had been told of the incident at the hotel on the afternoon before Stephanie Winstock's murder was true. An American lady had created a scene so embarrassing that in the end she had been asked to leave the premises.

'We know that it cannot have been Mademoiselle Winstock who caused this trouble,' Gautier commented, 'for she was still lunching with Madame Pitot.'

'I agree and by the description I was given of the woman, it certainly was not Stephanie Winstock.'

'In that case, it can only have been Pauline Fenn.'

The Salle Delacroix had been laid out for the wine-tasting with small circular tables, each seating six people, arranged in a semicircle round the room. In front of each place at the tables stood twelve empty wine glasses, a small notepad and a pencil but, Gautier was glad to see, nothing else. He knew that at some wine-tastings receptacles were provided into which tasters could spit the wine they had held in their mouths, but did not swallow. He had always felt that this was an affectation and that he could drink any reasonable number of glasses of wine without the taste of one seriously affecting his enjoyment of those that followed.

As they arrived he and the other guests had been affably received by Lucien Gambon and his elder son André. The younger son, Philippe, did not appear to be present and, when one of the guests asked whether they might have the pleasure of seeing him later, Lucien did not seem pleased.

'I have no idea why he is not here,' he said, 'he cannot be out seeing customers at this hour.'

Duthrey was one of the guests at the table with Gautier, together with two other journalists, Senderen from *Gil Blas* and a Madame Galland who contributed a regular column on wine to *Le Matin*. The two seats on either side of Gautier were empty and one, he assumed, had been intended for Lady Jane Shelford. It was only as Gambon was finishing his welcome, that a lady arrived hurriedly and sat down in one of the empty chairs. When he and the other men at the table began to rise, she motioned at them to remain seated. Her face seemed vaguely familiar, but Gautier could not remember having ever been introduced to her.

'I only arrived in Paris an hour ago,' she whispered, explaining her lateness to the others at the table, 'and had to go to my hotel to change.'

Lucien Gambon began his introduction to the tasting by telling those present that grapes had been cultivated in Burgundy since the earliest times and that by the twelfth century Burgundy wines were already famous. Bordeaux wines might be more widely drunk internationally today, but wines from Burgundy were more diverse, more complex and more consistent in quality. He was certain that in due course this would be recognized by all discerning lovers of fine wine and that then Burgundy wines would lead the world.

As he was speaking two waiters brought in an easel on which a large coloured map of eastern France had been affixed. Marked on the map were the five wine regions of Burgundy; Chablis to the north and below it the Côte d'Or, the Côte Chalonnaise, the Mâconnais and the Beaujolais. Gambon pointed them out and said that while during the evening everyone present would have an opportunity to sample at least one wine from all the five regions, the tasting would be concentrating largely on those from the Côte d'Or. The Côte d'Or might be divided into two parts, the Côte de Nuits and the Côte de Beaune and wines from both of these would dominate in the tasting.

'You must understand if I am being partisan in this issue,' he said smiling, 'but then Beaune has long been the home of my family and myself.'

Everyone laughed. Gambon was a polished speaker, articulate and genial. Gautier supposed that must all be part of his successful salesmanship. His son Philippe was also, on the evidence of a single meeting, also articulate, but André appeared more withdrawn. Once again Gautier had the feeling that he might be subdued by his father's presence.

As soon as Gambon finished his introduction, more waiters appeared, carrying bottles of white wine which they poured into the glasses, placing one in front of each guest. Gautier held up his glass to see the colour of the wine, for he knew that colour could be equally important as flavour to the quality of a wine. Gambon was also holding up his glass.

'Chablis,' he said, 'is one of the finest wines of Burgundy and one of the great white wines of France. It is made from Chardonnay grapes and owes its flavour as much to the soil of the region, chalk and limestone as to the grape. Look at the wine in your glasses. As you can see it is a pale yellow, edged with green. On your palate you will find it crisp and dry, but still fruity and fresh.'

The next wine to be tasted was also white, a Pouilly-Fuissé. This, Gambon told his guests, was without doubt the finest wine from the Mâconnais. He drew their attention to its colour, the yellow of straw, and its rich full-bodied bouquet. Here again it was the high limestone content of the soil that gave Pouilly-Fuissé its freshness, but at the same time a rich complexity of taste. Gautier accepted that Pouilly-Fuissé was a fine wine even though it had slightly too much acidity for his taste.

Two red wines were the next to be offered in the *degustation*; a Mercurey from the Côte Chalonnaise and a Fleurie from the Beaujolais. When the samples were given to him, Gautier and everyone at his table went through a kind of drill, holding up the glass, peering, then sniffing, sipping, rolling the wine round their mouths, and scribbling on their notepads. The guests had been encouraged to ask questions and several of them did. In the main the questions were practical; what was the age at which a particular wine should be drunk; how should wine be stored, to what type of cuisine was a particular wine suited.

After they had sampled the Fleurie, the woman sitting next to Gautier smiled at him and remarked, 'Well we have been taken through four of the five regions. For the rest of the evening, I guess we will be visiting out host's home town.' She spoke French with some fluency but with an Anglo-Saxon accent.

Gautier smiled back. 'Am I right in thinking that we have met before Madame?'

'Never, but I know you, Inspector Gautier, or at least your reputation. My name is Deborah Barclay.'

Gautier did not allow himself to be disconcerted. 'I thought you were in Dijon.'

'I was last night, but as I said earlier, I have just returned.'

The tasting continued as guests sampled a number of wines from the Côte de Nuits and the Côte de Beaune. Later Gautier would find it difficult to recall them all and certainly to distinguish between them. One which he found particularly to his personal taste was a Gevrey-Chambertin, a wine with a deep red colour made from pinot noir grapes. After that came a Vosne-Romanée and then a Volnay. Gambon spoke about all of them with a salesman's enthusiasm, but surprisingly the one wine about which he did not become lyrical was Château Perdrix.

'That seems an odd name for a château,' Mrs Barclay remarked. '*Perdrix* means partridge in English and what part do partridges play in wine-making?'

'It must be connected in some way with *oeil-de-perdrix*, the eye of the partridge,' Duthrey told her. 'That is an expression sometimes used to describe the very pale colour of certain white wines, but I have no idea how it originated.'

From time to time Gautier had glanced at Mrs Barclay and he began comparing her features with what he remembered of Lady Jane's. While Lady Jane's face, with its aquiline nose and craggy brow, reminded him of what many people might think to be that of a typical English aristocrat, Deborah Barclay's was smaller, less symmetrical but certainly more interesting and lively. He could imagine that she would be a difficult opponent in an argument. She looked younger than he had supposed she would be and he could imagine that she must have been unusually beautiful when she was a girl.

The *degustation* was approaching its end, the last wine had been tasted and Lucien Gambon was making a few final points. He told them again that it was not only the type of grape used which determined the flavour and quality of the wine. The *terroir*, the soil in which the grapes were grown was equally important, as were the climate, the location of the vineyard and, for example, whether or not it was sheltered from the winds. Finally he reminded his guests of the tremendous diversity of Burgundy wines.

'With so many fine wines to choose from, the name of the proprietor or négociant can be the best guarantee of quality.' He smiled. 'You will have noticed that on the labels of all the wines you have tasted today, the name of Lucien Gambon et Fils.'

Once again everyone laughed at his impudence and several people even applauded. Most of those present continued to sit where they were, finishing what was left in the bottles which the waiters had left on the tables. André was going from table to table unobtrusively taking orders.

'What did you think of the tasting?' Gautier called out to Duthrey.

'Excellent. I was impressed with our host's assessment of the wines. We were given a truly educational experience.'

'Monsieur Duthrey is a connoisseur. He has written an outstanding book on Burgundy wines,' Gautier told Mrs Barclay. Then he asked Duthrey, 'It would be a pity to let the evening end now, would it not? Shall we go and dine together?'

'That would be very pleasant, but I am expected at home. We have guests for dinner.'

The other journalists at the table also said that they had articles to write and must go back to the offices of their newspapers. Mrs Barclay looked at Gautier and smiled.

'I am not a journalist,' she said, 'so I have no office to visit!'

The restaurant on the Left Bank to which Gautier took Mrs Barclay was one he had visited only twice before, but one which he knew was small and chic. Many of those who dined there regularly were friends and this created a relaxed but sophisticated atmosphere, with comments and banter being exchanged from one table to another. He was sure the informal ambience would appeal to Americans, and he had another reason for taking Mrs Barclay there. He was inclined to believe that she had in effect compelled him to take her to dinner, in order to persuade him to do what he could to help Bishop Arkwright. If this were true he would hardly be justified in taking her to one of the more expensive restaurants on Paris.

When they arrived at the restaurant he had chosen, she seemed delighted and commented on its charm. Gautier had made up his mind that he would not ask her what had happened at the *instruction* in Dijon, nor raise the subject of Bishop Arkwright in any way. If Mrs Barclay had favours to ask of him, she would have to do it in her own way.

While they were choosing what they should order he asked her, 'Is this your first visit to France, Madame?'

'By no means. When my husband was alive he and I often came to Europe and always made a point of spending at least a little time in Paris.'

'In what line of business did your husband work?'

'I suppose you would call him an industrialist. His company manufactured automobiles.'

'Do you have children?'

'We had two boys, twins, but both were killed in an automobile accident soon after their eighteenth birthday.'

For a moment Mrs Barclay's eyes, which had seemed to be always bright and challenging, clouded with sadness. Suddenly for the first time since they had met, Gautier felt a sympathy for her, sympathy and a touch of guilt. He had been judging her simply on what he had heard of her association with Bishop Arkwright; a ruthless, self-important bigot. Was it possible that travelling with the man and being used by him was no more than an escape ftom the loneliness suffered by an ageing woman whom life had treated harshly?

To accompany their dinner he ordered a bottle of Clos de Vougeot, a more expensive wine than those he would normally drink, but one which he knew came from a château not far from Gambon's home. He had noticed that at that evening's tasting Mrs Barclay had placed an order for a dozen cases of the wines to which they had been introduced, which would be shipped to her home on Long Island. He was curious to know how Arkwright had been able to reconcile her appreciation of wine with his own condemnation of all drink.

'How did you come to be invited to this evening's tasting?' he asked her. 'Have you met Lucien Gambon before?'

'Not Monsieur Gambon himself but during a visit to Paris a year or two ago I was introduced to his son Philippe, a singularly charming young man.'

'He was not there this evening.'

'No. I feel sorry for him. He has had many disappointments in his life. He persuaded his father to allow him to set up an office in Paris, but he is still discontented. He has no social standing here, you understand. If one is not accepted by the great aristocratic families, one is nothing. And yet he had given up the chance of marrying a rich Irish girl to come to Paris.'

Mrs Barclay quickly seemed to lose interest in Philippe Gambon and she began telling Gautier about her husband and how he ran his automobile factory. He was one of those leaders of industry in America, she told him, who supported temperance. In his experience excessive drinking by workmen was one of the major problems facing industry. Drunkenness led to poor time-keeping, shoddy work and accidents on the shop floor. A sober workforce would bring many benefits to industry, including higher productivity and better profits. So he and the owners of large corporations encouraged temperance campaigns and made substantial contributions to temperance organizations.

'But he did not give up drinking himself?' Gautier asked her.

'Never. Sam enjoyed a couple of Bourbons every evening and the cocktail cabinet at home was always well stocked. He knew that it was in the saloons where working men got drunk. That was why he supported the Anti-Saloon League and I decided I should continue to support it after he died.'

In spite of his earlier resolve, Gautier could not resist taking the opening she had given him. 'And is that why you are funding Bishop Arkwright's trip to Europe?'

'Yes. He heard I was coming to France and asked whether I would allow him to accompany me – and meet all his expenses of course!' She paused, looked at him searchingly and then added, 'I hope you are not one of those who believe I am his mistress.'

'Are you not?'

'Please credit me with more taste than that! As you must have noticed, Bishop Arkwright is not an attractive man. He also has a loyal wife back home. I offered to pay her expenses if she came with him to France, but he would not bring her.'

'Did he not tell the police at Dijon that he had spent the whole night of the murder with you?'

'He did and like a fool I did not deny it at the time. He asked me not to because he was afraid that the police might stop him returning to Paris. It seemed a harmless deception. After all the man, a priest, could never commit murder, could he?'

'And when you were questioned by Judge Jolivet in Dijon this morning you told the truth?' Gautier guessed.

'I had to, of course. I would not commit perjury for Bishop Arkwright.'

Gautier was inclined to believe Mrs Barclay. She was well brought up and educated, but like many women of her background she behaved not foolishly, but unthinkingly. If a situation seemed of little consequence to her she was careless with the truth and would lie if she were asked to, but even so she had her own morality.

'I am glad he is not in Paris,' she continued. 'When he heard that I had been invited to this wine tasting he wanted to come as my guest. I refused of course. Can you imagine what a scene he would have created?'

'He might well have come along without an invitation.'

'Very possibly, especially if he knew journalists would be there. The man is a fool. He believes that publicity, any publicity, can only further the cause of temperance and therefore his own career.'

Gautier's slender hope that he might learn something from Deborah Barclay that would throw some light on the murder of Michael O'Flynn or that of Stephanie Winstock was not realized. They spent the remainder of the evening talking of France, of its history, of contemporary politics, of the changing face of Paris. Deborah was surprisingly knowledgeable about French culture and eager to know more.

When he was taking her back to the Hôtel Cheltenham in a fiacre, he asked her 'How much longer is Bishop Arkwright staying in Europe?'

'He is due to return to the States in two days' time; that is if the police will allow him to leave. The sooner the better I say.'

'Are you travelling together?'

'Certainly not! Never again. I plan to stay on in Paris for at least another week.' She reached out and placed a hand on his arm. 'I have enjoyed this evening so much Inspector. Will I see you again?'

Gautier had also enjoyed the evening but he had no intention of committing himself.

'I hope so, but it is likely that I will have to go to Dijon shortly.'

12

Next morning transcripts of the previous day's proceedings at the *instruction* lay on Gautier's desk, just as Judge Loubet had promised. They made dull reading, giving a picture of the events following the discovery in the pension of Stephanie Winstock's dead body and little more. Gautier flicked through them, looking for the questions and answers which he knew would interest him. He found them in the afternoon's proceedings.

QUESTION: You keep a record of the arrival of every guest at your establishment do you not?

BRISSART: We do of course, your honour.

QUESTION: And does this show the time of their arrival?

BRISSART: Not the exact time, but we would know from the register whether a guest arrived in the morning, afternoon or evening.

QUESTION: Nothing more precise than that?

BRISSART: No, but my wife or I would probably remember at roughly what hour any particular guest arrived.

QUESTION: We are interested in the man Robinet. Can you tell us at what time he arrived.

BRISSART: My wife and I have discussed that. We believe he arrived and asked for a room at about five in the afternoon.

QUESTION: As late as that? It appears then that he had not booked a room in advance. Is that customary?

BRISSART: Yes, your honour. At this time of the year very often 'casuals' as we call them, will arrive asking for a room until quite late in the evening.

The questioning continued, first of Brissart and then of his wife, without adding much about Robinet that the police did not already know. The man's behaviour, not sleeping in his bed and slipping out of the pension unnoticed, made him the obvious suspect for the murder of Stephanie Winstock. He must have gone to the pension for that purpose, which meant that he had known where she was staying. Efforts to trace him had so far produced no results and they could be stepped up, with more men being allocated to the search, but with so little being known about the man, the chances of success would be small. Gautier sent for Surat.

'What have we been doing to find this man Robinet?' he asked him.

'Our enquiries in Belgium have produced nothing, so men are going round the small hotels and pensions in Paris asking if they know anything of such a man.'

'They are probably wasting their time. I have another idea, just an idea, nothing more, but it could be worth exploring. We will start at the Hôtel Trumpington.'

On the way to the hotel he explained to Surat that such evidence as they had, suggested that the murder of Stephanie Winstock had been planned and yet, when committing it, the murderer had been assisted by chance to a remarkable extent. He must have waited in the pension for his victim to arrive in her room and then stabbed her, but she had been sharing a room and it was purely by chance that she had been alone. One might have expected that her secretary would have been with her or waiting for her when she returned to their room. Also by chance the room next to the one occupied by the two women had been vacant. It had provided the killer with a place where he could dispose of his weapon and might well have been where he had waited for his victim to return to her room.

'I am beginning to believe,' Gautier said, 'that Robinet, or whoever the murderer was, knew that Winstock was living in the pension and very little more about her. He may never even have seen her before. The murder appears to be motiveless and you know as well as I do what the great majority of such killings turn out to be.'

'Paid assassinations?'

'Precisely. One can have someone killed in Paris for as little as a hundred francs.'

'But who would wish to have this woman killed?

'I have no idea yet, but I believe we might find a clue to that at the Hôtel Trumpington.'

At the hotel they were taken to see the manager in his office. Gautier knew most of the managers of the leading hotels in Paris at least slightly and could rely on their cooperation in any investigations he might be making. The Hôtel Trumpington, he knew, was well run and was seldom involved even indirectly in any criminal matters. When Gautier told him that he wished to know more about the fracas at the hotel caused by an American woman the previous week, the manager shrugged.

'It was embarrassing mothing more. The woman behaved very badly.'

'Did she by any chance say where she was staying?'

'She did and more than once. She said that she and her secretary were staying in some pension – I forget the name – and said how comfortable it was and how much better managed than this hotel.'

'And would other people have heard what she was saying?'

'Certainly. Anyone in the lobby would have heard. In my view she was deliberately trying to insult the hotel. I cannot think why.'

'We are looking for a man who might have been here, a man named Robinet.'

The manager listened while Gautier gave him a sketchy description of Robinet, put together from what the staff and guests at the pension had said. Then he shook his head.

'We have no one staying here who fits that description.'

'Would you let us see your list of guests for that time?'

The manager produced two lists of registrations, one for the night preceding Winstock's murder and the other for the following night. Only one name meant anything to Gautier; that of a Lucien Gambon from Beaune.

'Is that Monsieur Gambon the *négociant-en-vins*?' Gautier asked.

'Yes, Inspector. He had arrived by train at midday and booked in during the afternoon. He told me that he and his son would be visiting customers in Paris and also checking the arrangements for a wine tasting they would be holding at the Salle Delacroix.'

'Do you know whether he was in the lobby when the American woman was misbehaving?'

The manager frowned. 'I am not sure. No, wait! I remember now that he was. He was waiting for his son to collect him and in rather a bad temper, because his son was late.'

The office of the Wilmington Detective Agency was on the fourth floor of an unprepossessing building in an unprepossessing part of

Paris, not far from Belleville. Inside the office Gautier and Surat found a man in his shirt sleeves and wearing a green eyeshade seated at a desk. When they introduced themselves as police officers, the man, whose name was Parker, seemed to become defensive in attitude.

Gautier tried to reassure him. 'We are hoping, Monsieur, that your agency can help us. It is a matter of a scoundrel who has been swindling rich ladies out of large sums of money.'

'I know nothing of any such affair.'

'We have been told that a wealthy American lady, a Madame Harrington from New York, employed your agency to discover the identity of this rogue.'

'After she had parted with the money?'

'Unfortunately yes. A very large sum.'

'There you are!' Parker said. 'Shutting the stable door! Women only come to us when the damage has been done and then they ask us to pick up the pieces.' The mixed metaphors, translated literally into the man's atrocious French, might at any other time have been amusing.

'Then you knew of this woman?'

'Inspector, almost all of our clients are women. They ask us to spy on their husbands, looking for evidence of infidelity, or to protect them in their own indiscretions with lovers. As I told you, I have no recollection of any such case and in any event I cannot pass on to you any confidential information given to our detectives by our clients.'

'Are you saying that you did not work on such a case yourself?'

'I never handle any investigations myself,' Parker replied stubbornly. 'My French is not good enough. All our leg-work is done by the French detectives on our staff. I just manage the agency.'

'And you know nothing of this woman Harrington?' Gautier persisted. Any detective agency operating in Paris would need the co-operation of the Sûreté to survive and Parker should be made aware of this fact. 'We know for a fact that she engaged your agency.'

'Now that you remind me of it, the name is familiar,' Parker said grudgingly. 'We conducted enquiries for a Mrs Harrington of New York some weeks ago. It was a trifling matter.'

'And who carried out the inquiries?'

'One of our detectives named Crozier.'

'We would like to speak with him.'

'He is no longer on our staff. The man was a rogue himself, obviously dishonest; never gave us any information on this client, nor produced any fees. I was planning to fire him, but he left without giving me any warning, just failed to turn up one day.'

'When was this?'

'I forget which day it was, but with Crozier one never knew whether he was working for us or not.'

Gautier was sure the man was lying and he realized that this avenue of enquiry was leading nowhere. With some reluctance the manager gave them a description of the French detective Crozier. It was one which might have matched that of Robinet, but equally it could have fitted any number of men in Paris.

When Gautier returned to Sûreté headquarters with Surat, he found a visitor waiting to see him. André Gambon had arrived a few minutes earlier and was told he might wait since the Chief Inspector was not expected to be long. Gambon was carrying two packages.

'My father sent me here to apologize, Inspector,' he said.

'For what?'

'On behalf of my brother Philippe. As you will have noticed, he was not at our wine-tasting yesterday evening.'

'Did that matter?' Gautier replied. 'You and your father conducted the tasting with great skill and panache. I learnt a tremendous amount, as I am sure the other guests did.'

'Even so, as Philippe invited you he should have been there.'

'I am sure he had a good reason for his absence.'

'He had a reason of course. Apparently some days ago he attended a reunion dinner with some of the friends he made in the army, while he was doing his military service. It was in fact on the Saturday when the banquet of the *Confrérie* was being held in Dijon.'

André explained that Philippe and his army friends held a reunion once a year, always on a Saturday. On this last occasion they had agreed to hold a further meeting to celebrate the engagement of one of their number. As at all their reunions they had been drinking freely and Philippe had not realized that this celebration was to be held on a Tuesday, the same evening as the wine-tasting which his father had arranged. Indeed he had forgotten all about the celebration and it was only when a friend had telephoned him in the late afternoon of the Tuesday, that he remembered his commitment. He had felt obliged to attend and had tried to telephone his father to explain, but Lucien and André were already on their way from Dijon. He had left a message at the Salle Delacroix, but it had not been passed on.

'You can understand now why my father was so annoyed,' André concluded.

'Your brother's excuse is plausible and in any case no harm was done. The tasting was most enjoyable,' Gautier replied, though he wondered why André had felt to obliged to explain Philippe's absence at such length.

'Whatever the reason, it was gross discourtesy,' André said, 'and as a token of our family's regret I have brought these two bottles of wine. They are both wines you tasted yesterday.' He smiled. 'One is for you and the other for your charming companion.'

Gautier realized that he must be referring to Mrs Barclay. 'The American lady was not my companion. We happened to be seated next to each other.'

'But you left together. Did you not take her out to dine?'

Gautier shrugged to show that taking Mrs Barclay to dinner had no special significance and was merely a courtesy. He saw no reason why he should account for his actions to Gambon. The man could not have come to the Sûreté merely to deliver two bottles of wine. No doubt the reason for his visit would become clear in due course.

'You do not mind taking her the wine, do you?' André asked.

'I shall have both bottles delivered to her hotel. As a police officer, you understand, I cannot accept gifts myself.'

Gambon did not appear to object to what Gautier had suggested. He said, 'We were relieved when she arrived at the tasting on her own. We were afraid that she might have brought her travelling companion, the bishop, as her guest.'

'If she had, he would have ruined your tasting. You must have heard what he did at the banquet of the Confrérie in Dijon.'

Gambon smiled again. He appeared relaxed and in a good humour, One had the impression that away from the inhibiting presence of his father, he had just as much charm as his brother, perhaps even more.

'We had taken precautions to see that did not happen.'

It was Gautier's turn to smile. 'Was that the reason I was invited? To guarantee his good behaviour?'

'Not at all. We learnt of your interest in wine when he met you at the railway station in Dijon.' Gambon paused, thinking no doubt of how he could steer the conversation towards whatever the purpose of his visit might be. Eventually he asked, 'Have you been to Dijon again since that day? I understand that you were helping the local police with their enquiries into the death of Michael O'Flynn.'

'They really do not need any help from me.'

'Why not? There are striking similarities between the killing of O'Flynn and that of the American disciple of temperance, Stephanie Winstock. Both were viciously stabbed and both in their bedrooms.'

André's questions were beginning to irritate Gautier. He must be shown that any attempts to influence a police investigation would not be tolerated. The words of a firm rebuff were forming in his mind, but he was spared the need to give one when the Prefect of Police came into the room. Gautier was surprised. The Prefect had never been in his office before and he was rarely in Sûreté headquarters at all. On this occasion one could only assume that he had been discussing policy matters with the Director General and had taken the opportunity to call in on Gautier.

'You know Monsieur André Gainbon do you not, Monsieur le Préfet?' Gautier said, going through the motions of an introduction although he knew one would probably not be needed.

'Indeed. I have known André since he was a lad.' The Prefect smiled and then added, 'You must forgive me gentlemen, for disturbing you. I came to ask you, Gautier, if you could take the first train to Dijon this afternoon. A room has been reserved for you at the Hostellerie du Chapeau Rouge.'

On the train heading for Dijon, Gautier wondered what reason the Prefect had for sending him there and supposed it must be connected with the *instruction* which Judge Jolivet was conducting and which must now be on its third day. Perhaps Joséphine O'Flynn was shortly due to appear before the judge and Gautier was being sent to Dijon to boost her morale. On his way to the Gare du Lyon he had called in at the Hôtel Cheltenham to give

Mrs Barclay the two bottles of wine which Philippe Gambon had brought to his office. She had been in the hotel's dining-room, just about to lunch and had seemed delighted to see him.

'I thought you were going to Dijon,' she had said.

'I am on my way there.'

'Then you must join me in an apéritif first.'

A waiter had brought them each a glass of a *vin doux naturel* to sip as they chatted at the table.

'Do you have any messages for me to take to Bishop Arkwright?' Gautier had asked her mischievously.

'Tell him to stay in Dijon. I am just beginning to enjoy myself in Paris on my own.'

He had been curious to know why Judge Jolivet had allowed her to return to Paris while Arkwright was being detained in Dijon, but she was in too frivolous a mood for serious conversation and seemed determined to flirt with him. So he had learnt nothing of any significance about the *instruction* before he had to leave to catch his train. That did not worry him, for he had no doubt that Inspector Le Harivel would let him have transcripts of each day's proceedings to study if he so wished. In any case he was more interested to know what role the Prefect of Police was playing in the affair.

When he reached Dijon he walked from the station to the hotel and was once again struck by the charm of the town, its sense of history and culture. The excitement surrounding a brutal murder did not seem in any way to have disturbed its peaceful calm. At the hotel the concierge confirmed that a room had been reserved for him and told him that an automobile would be collecting him in an hour's time to drive him to the Château Perdrix.

While he was still talking to the concierge he heard his name called out behind him. He turned and saw Bishop Arkwright approaching.

'So it was you, Inspector Gautier,' the bishop shouted angrily. 'I might have known that you were behind this!'

'Monsieur?'

'The police are insisting that I remain in Dijon. Are you seriously suggesting that I may have murdered that wine merchant? I am a minister of God!'

'The investigation of this crime is a matter for the Dijon police. I have no competence in the affair.'

'I refuse to believe that. On what grounds am I being held here?'

'One reason may be that you lied to the police.'

'This is all a conspiracy contrived by that woman Winstock and the foreigners who fund and support her. Can you not see that? America is being ravished by Catholics and foreigners. Why, even her name betrays her origins!'

Gautier's frown may have shown that he found it difficult to follow this tortuous argument, for Arkwright stormed on, 'Winstock is a German name; German and Jewish; a corruption of Weinstock. And now by attacking me, she is serving the interests of that great destroyer, wine. Ironic is it not?

'Stephanie Winstock is not the reason why the police are detaining you in Dijon,' Gautier said.

Bishop Arkwright paid no attention but ranted on, first attacking his enemies, then protesting his innocence, reminding Gautier of his holy calling and invoking God to be his witness. Eventually, wearying of his tirade, he switched to a more practical matter. 'Have you any idea what this charade is costing me? The programme of my European tour has been interrupted, the sermons I was to give have been cancelled. I warn you, Gautier, you will have to pay for this. I shall sue for compensation.'

Gautier looked at him calmly. 'For any legal claim to be successful you would have had to prove a financial loss.'

'Well?'

'I understand that the expenses of your visit to Europe are all being met by your patron, Mrs Barclay.'

The apartments of the O'Flynn family were at the back of the Château Perdrix, on the other side of the great hall and away from the *chai* where the wine was made and the *caves* where it was stored. When he arrived there he was taken up to the drawing room where Joséphine O'Flynn and her two daughters were waiting for him. Cara, the elder daughter, with her dark hair and soulful eyes, was clearly of Irish descent. Her sister Bronagh, even though her hair was red, had a pretty, sharp-featured face that seemed to Gautier unmistakably French. In neither of them could he see any sign of the discontent which lingered, permanently it seemed, in their mother's expression.

'As you have come all this way,' Madame O'Flynn said, 'we felt we must give you dinner. There is nowhere in Dijon where one can eat well.'

'Are you a friend of Uncle Dodi?' Cara asked Gautier.

'She means the Prefect of Police,' Madame O'Flynn explained. 'The girls have treated him as an uncle ever since they were tiny.'

'We are not exactly friends. I work for him.'

'The you must live in Paris,' Bronagh said and when he had admitted that he did, she demanded, 'Tell us about Paris.'

'Yes, you must,' Cara insisted. 'Do you know we have only ever been taken to Paris three or four times and then never for more than a day or two. Even Uncle Dodi is not allowed to invite us.'

The nickname seemed inappropriate for a man of such style and sophistication as the Prefect and Gautier resolved that he must never say anything which would show him that he had been told it. He began talking about Paris, answering the girls' questions on the city's theatres, circuses, music halls and restaurants.

They wanted to hear about the salacious novels of Colette and the new artists of Montmartre who were shocking the bourgeoisie, Their mother listened indulgently as the conversation continued over dinner. As they talked Gautier was struck by the relaxed and amiable atmosphere. The father of the family had been dead for not much more than a week, yet no one mentioned his name and one could not help feeling that he was not greatly missed.

When the meal was over, the two girls left the table to return to their own rooms. Gautier could not help thinking that this must have been prearranged, so as to leave him alone with their mother and that now she would tell him why she had invited him to her château that evening. When they were leaving and as he was kissing their hands, Cara impulsively leant forward and kissed him on the cheek. It was a gesture often made by young children but not by girls in their twenties.

Cara, he decided, would have many admirers. Although she was not strikingly pretty, she had an appeal rare among women but compelling. When she looked into a man's eyes he became aware of an unspoken promise; a promise that she lived in her own thrilling, seductive world into which he, and only he, might join her whenever he chose.

When the girls had left, Madame O'Flynn said to him, 'What do you think of my daughters?'

'Charming! They are both absolutely charming.'

'But unmarried. It's absurd. Do you not agree?'

Gautier did not know what to reply. He had not been expecting questions about her daughters, but about the investigations into the murder of her husband. He temporized. 'At least you still have them at home to support you at this difficult time.'

Madame O'Flynn made a noise to show her disdain for the remark. 'I would be happier if they were married and supporting their own children.' She looked at him. 'What do you think of the

Gambon boys?' He could not immediately think of a reply which would be entirely honest, but she was evidently not interested in his opinion, for she continued, 'They are both mad about the girls. My daughters are both admired and respected locally, even if they do not have money. We should have married them off years ago.'

'Is that what you are planning?'

She shrugged. 'It depends on what conclusion Judge Jolivet reaches after his examination. Will anyone still wish to marry into the O'Flynn family?'

'Surely nothing he decides can impugn the integrity of your family?'

She hesitated, but only briefly. 'Let me put it this way, Inspector Gautier. I shall be appearing at the judicial examination tomorrow and I would prefer it if I were not asked where I was on the night my husband was murdered.'

'I understood you were at home here in the château.'

'I was, but not alone. The Gambon brothers were here with us.'

'Both of them?'

'Yes. Let me be honest, Inspector. As I told you when we last met, I was intending to leave my husband. The girls would of course come with me. They could not be left here at the château, but I would not be able to support them for ever. I had to be assured of their future, so that evening the five of us were planning a little conspiracy.'

'You were discussing their marriages?'

'Exactly. Bronagh would marry Philippe and Cara would marry André, but that was to be a secret for the time being and I would be grateful if you would not mention it to anyone.'

Gautier wondered why he was being told this. Was this the reason why he had been sent down to Dijon from Paris? If so the Prefect of Police must be involved or at least be privy to Madame

O'Flynn's secret. Before he could make any comment she rose from the dining-table.

'We cannot talk here,' she said, 'let us find somewhere more comfortable.'

He followed her out of the room and up a flight of stairs to a much smaller room which could only be her boudoir. A decanter of cognac was standing on a small table by one wall and she poured two glasses, one of which she handed to him. Then she went and sat on a *chaise-longue* in the centre of the room and pointed to a chair beside it.

'We will be more comfortable here, do you not agree?' she said.

Gautier made no reply. He was reluctant to believe it, but the scene she was creating had all the classic symptoms of a seduction as depicted in a play by Dumas *fils*. Could she really be hoping that she could tempt him into some indiscretion, into playing some part in a scheme she had in mind? The idea seemed absurd. He took the coward's way out and waited for her to act.

'What I am afraid of,' she said at last, 'is that what I say before Judge Jolivet tomorrow might embarrass the Prefect.'

'I cannot see how it possibly could, Madame.'

She smiled. 'I imagine he feels the same way or why else did he ask you to come down to Dijon? You must be in a position to influence the course that Judge Jolivet takes in his examination tomorrow.'

'The Sûreté has no competence in what is a local matter,' he replied stubbornly.

'Are you sure of that?'

'The Prefect of Police would, I know, agree with me.'

Gautier detected a sudden change in Madame O'Flynn's attitude. Either she had lost heart or had gone as far as she was willing to go, leaving him with unspoken promises of favours to come if he were to do what she had suggested.

'Thank you for coming to see me this evening, Inspector,' she said. 'I feel greatly reassured after our talk.' Gautier recognized that this was a dismissal and rose from his chair. 'The chauffeur is waiting and will drive you back to your hotel. I shall expect to see you at the examination tomorrow.'

13

Two telegrams arrived for Gautier at the hotel next morning. He had enjoyed the luxury of a late breakfast in his bedroom because he had been told that Judge Jolivet insisted that the first sessions of his instruction should not begin every morning until ten o'clock. The people of Dijon, he had decided, lived life at a much gentler pacc than those of Paris.

The first telegram, which he realized must have been despatched the previous evening, was from Ingrid. It read:

> THE WASHINGTON POST HAVE GIVEN ME AN ASSIGNMENT TO WORK FOR A MONTH AS REPLACEMENT FOR THEIR REGULAR CORRESPONDENT IN RIO DE JANEIRO WHO HAS HAD TO BE RECALLED FOR PERSONAL REASONS. THE ASSIGNMENT IS IN EFFECT A TRIAL AND IF SATISFACTORY I WILL BE GIVEN A REGULAR POSTING IN EUROPE. HOPE MY ABSENCE HAS CREATED A VOID IN YOUR LIFE BUT DOUBT IT.
>
> INGRID.

Gautier smiled when he read the telegram. The flippant little remark at the end of the message was typical of Ingrid. She would certainly succeed in this trial assignment, for she was a more than competent journalist and Portuguese was one of the seven languages which she spoke fluently.

The second telegram, which contained no sentimental messages, was from Surat. It reported that a man had been found murdered in Paris's 20th arrondissement. The murdered man had been shot by a pistol at close range, and his description matched that of Crozier, the former operative of the Wilmington Detective Agency. An unusually large sum of money had been found on the person of the murdered man.

Because of the interest that O'Flynn's death had aroused and the number of witnesses that were being called, Judge Jolivet's *instruction* was being held in a room at the Hostellerie du Chapeau Rouge. After coming down from his room, Gautier was wondering how he should fill in the time before it began, when he saw Inspector Le Harivel waiting for him in the hotel lobby. Le Harivel had brought with him for Gautier a summary of what had happened on the two previous days and a list of the witnesses to be called that morning. Gautier glanced through the papers quickly and since there were still twenty minutes before Judge Jolivet arrived, he and Le Harivel had taken a stroll though the streets surrounding the hotel.

'As you will see from those papers,' Le Harivel said, 'we have made little progress in establishing who killed O'Flynn. Right from the start our difficulty has been to come up with a plausible motive for the murder.'

Gautier was tempted to tell him that in Paris the Sûreté was faced with the same problem of a seemingly motiveless killing. He did not, because from there it would only be a short step towards wondering whether the two murders were related and that might easily begin to cloud their thinking.

'How has Bishop Arkwright been behaving?' he asked Le Harivel.

'The man is a fool; his own worst enemy. He told a lie, thinking it would be an easy way out of becoming involved in a police investigation and now, instead of admitting the lie, he keeps on bursting into a tirade of temperance propaganda. Yesterday the judge lost patience, stopped questioning him and told him he would have to return this morning.'

'But his companion Mrs Barclay was allowed to return to Paris?'

'Yes. Her honesty and frankness made a very good impression on Judge Jolivet. It is obvious that she had no part in the murder.'

'And when will Madame O'Flynn be asked to give her evidence?'

'That depends on how long the questioning of Bishop Arkwright continues. Not later than early this afternoon I would think. The judge will not wish to inconvenience Madame O'Flynn for too long. After all she is only being asked to give evidence as a matter of form.'

Here was another indication, Gautier thought, that provincials took a different attitude from Parisians even in matters of law. The widow of a prominent businessman was being given, if not preferential treatment, then at least a special courtesy. He would be looking forward to seeing whether Madame O'Flynn took advantage of this feudal mark of respect.

Le Harivel had only one more thing to tell him about the investigations which the Dijon police had been conducting into the murder. On the evidence that had been collected so far, it had been decided that Armand Pascal should not be treated as a suspect and he was not being required to give evidence.

When they reached the room in which the *instruction* was being held, it was beginning to fill up with police officers and witnesses. Presently Judge Jolivet arrived and took his place at a table before which stood the chairs where the witnesses would sit as they were being questioned. Le Harivel sat on one side of him and on the other were the two clerks who would record the questions he asked and the replies he was given.

Bishop Arkwright arrived in the room a minute or two after the judge and Gautier wondered whether his late arrival was deliberate, calculated to show his contempt for the legal process to which he was being subjected. His face, which at any time looked hard and unyielding, was set in lines of stubborn determination.

'Monsieur,' Jolivet began politely enough, 'you were asked yesterday to give an account of your movements in the hours leading up to and immediately after midnight on the night of the unlawful killing of Monsieur Michael O'Flynn. We are ready to receive that account now.'

'I was carrying out my duties as a minister of God.'

'Please be more explicit, Monsieur.'

'I attended an assembly in the château of the deceased and attempted to restrain those present from the sin they were committing, when introducing initiates to the sins of the flesh and the perils of intoxication.'

'This court is not concerned with your religious pretensions. When did you reach your hotel and what did you do on your arrival?'

Arkwright ignored the question. He stood up and waved his hands in the direction of everyone in the room. 'You are all guilty! All of you makers and purveyors of the noxious invention of the devil, wine!' he shouted. 'You are guilty of a sin worse than fornication.'

Judge Jolivet waited for him to finish. Then he said very quietly, 'Monsieur Arkwright, if you do not stop behaving in this manner, you will be arrested, taken away and kept in prison, until you recognize my authority and begin to answer my questions.'

This time his words and his manner had an effect. Arkwright sat down, sulking. In reply to Jolivet's questions he admitted that he had returned to the Hostellerie du Chapeau Rouge soon after midnight on the night of O'Flynn's murder, gone to his room alone, slept and remained there until his *petit déjeuner* had been brought up and he had been made aware of the murder.

More questions followed, to all of which he replied grudgingly but rationally. Eventually the judge seemed satisfied. 'You may leave this examination now, Monsieur and you may return to Paris. Indeed the town of Dijon will not be sorry to see you depart. However I would caution you against causing any trouble for the law, in which case your behaviour at this examination would be taken into account.'

The questioning of Joséphine O'Flynn began that afternoon as soon as Jolivet and the other officials had returned from a leisurely lunch. She arrived heavily veiled and was treated by Jolivet with the greatest courtesy. In answer to his questions, she said that she had been at home at the Château Perdrix with her daughters on the night of her husband's death. The reason he had given for deciding to spend the night in Dijon had been simply to avoid the journey home, since he had expected that his official duties in connection with the *Confrérie des Chevaliers du Tastevin*, which were to take him to Dijon after the banquet, would detain him into the early hours of the morning. She spoke quietly and firmly, but Gautier would have liked to have been able to see her face as she did so.

The judge asked her more questions. Did she know of anyone who might have wished to kill her husband? Was she aware of any threats that had been made on his life? Had he seemed in any way troubled when he left their château on the morning of his death? Another question, which only the French, Gautier decided, would feel had to be asked, touched on the possibility of infidelity. Jolivet asked it as tactfully as he could. Was it in any way possible that her husband had at any time, perhaps even in the distant past, enjoyed a liaison with another woman? After all, it appeared certain that he must have known the person to whom he opened the door of his room that night and who then murdered him. A lesser woman might have been indignant at the question, but Madame O'Flynn gave an honest reply. If her husband had ever been unfaithful, she said, she was not aware of it.

While she was replying, Gautier noticed the Prefect of Police arrive. He slipped into the room unostentatiously, glanced towards Gautier but did not nod. When Jolivet had no more questions to ask Madame O'Flynn, he allowed her to leave, getting up and escorting her to the door in a gesture of sympathy as much as chivalry.

More witnesses were then paraded for questioning. The chambermaid at the hotel who had found O'Flynn's body and the concierge whom she had called to the scene, had already given their evidence at the start of the *instruction*. One witness whom Jolivet questioned now, was the doctor who had been called to the hotel and who had examined the body. He should have given his evidence much earlier in the proceedings, but he had been stricken down by a *grippe* and even now wheezed and muttered hoarsely as he spoke.

He had little of real value to offer. The cause of the victim's death, he said, had been a single blow to the heart. Death had been instantaneous. The weapon may have been a knife or dagger and the thrust had been expertly delivered. He could not be certain but it appeared likely that the assailant had been of much the same height as his victim, neither much taller nor much shorter. As he listened to what the doctor had to say, Gautier could not help remembering the evidence of another doctor at the *instruction* in Paris. The similarities between the murder of Stephanie Winstock and that of O'Flynn were plain, but the same could be said of a score of murders committed every month in Paris.

When Judge Jolivet had decided to end his examination for the day and Gautier was leaving the room, the Prefect approached him.

'I need to have a word with you Gautier.'

'Of course, Monsieur. Back at the hotel?'

'No. I am not staying there. There is a café called Le Jaquot a short walk from here behind the cathedral. I will meet you there in fifteen minutes.'

He left the room, hurriedly it seemed. Gautier also left and went up to his room in the hotel, where he drafted a telegram to the Sûreté in Paris. In it he instructed Surat, that he should arrange for Parker, the manager of the Wilmington Detective Agency, to be shown the body of the latest murder victim. If he confirmed that it was Crozier, then Surat should find out all he could about the man; where in Paris he lived, whether he had a family, whether he had any previous convictions for criminal offences. Any information gathered should be telegraphed to Inspector Gautier at once.

As he gave the telegram to the concierge to have it sent, Gautier realized that he need not have given these instructions. Surat was quite capable of taking the necessary routine steps in this latest murder and might well have already taken them. What made him act was a kind of frustration, a feeling that he was no more than a spectator at Dijon in a criminal case into which he had been drawn simply by chance, by Duthrey's invitation to attend a banquet of the *Confrérie des Chevaliers du Tastevin*.

He found the Café Jaquot without difficulty and as he was waiting there, began to speculate on why the Prefect of Police had made him come to Dijon and why he himself was there. From what he had been told the Prefect may have had some form of romantic relationship with Joséphine O'Flynn before she married and it would be easy now to read some sinister motive behind his arrival in Dijon so soon after her husband's death, but he knew the man. Subtle he certainly was and he could in his own way be devious, but Gautier could not believe that he would ever manipulate the law to his own advantage or that of his friends.

When the Prefect arrived, he seemed quietly pleased with himself. He ordered a bottle of wine for them to share and then he said, 'I want to thank you, Gautier, for coming down here.'

'Monsieur?'

'Judge Jolivet's judicial examination passed off very well, I think.'

'He is no closer to establishing who killed Michael O'Flynn.'

The Prefect shrugged. 'Even so. And having you here has been most reassuring for Madame O'Flynn.'

'It is kind of you to say so, Monsieur.' Gautier had to work hard to keep the faintest touch of sarcasm out of his remark. 'And should I now return to Paris?'

'Not yet. There may still be surprises in tomorrow's proceedings. Besides, tomorrow evening there will be the wake. The O'Flynn family would, I know, like you to be there.'

'A wake, Monsieur?' The Prefect had used the English word which Gautier had never heard before.

'It is the traditional way in which the Irish honour their dead, a vigil if you like. I understand that in his will Michael stipulated that when he died a wake should be held for him.'

When he sat down to dine alone in the hotel that evening, Gautier was not thinking of Michael O'Flynn's murder, but of Ingrid. Her telegram had told him that she would be away for another four weeks and that afterwards she was expecting a permanent posting in Europe. He could understand her ambition to be one of the *Washington Post*'s correspondents. The number of women journalists in France and indeed in Europe was small and in the main they were employed only to contribute regular columns on a limited range of topics; fashion was one, but also books, drama and cultural activities. It seemed likely now that the *Washington Post* would take Ingrid on to its European staff, but that did not necessarily mean she would be working in France. French was only one of the seven languages which she spoke fluently and the *Post* might well prefer to send her to her native Holland. Another possibility was Berlin, where political activity was intense, with Germany likely to be a protagonist in the European war that everyone was beginning to expect.

Gautier's friendship with Ingrid had been brief and the passion they had shared even briefer. Ever since his wife had died, he had enjoyed attachments with a succession of women, each of whom had slipped in and out of his life without leaving any permanent mark and he was beginning to believe sadly that Ingrid might be another. He was looking at the evening's dinner menu, when he heard a woman's voice.

'Would you mind if I joined you, Inspector?'

He looked up and was surprised to see that the woman was Mrs Barclay.

'What are you doing here?' he asked her. 'I thought you were in Paris.'

'Is that your way of inviting me to dine with you?'

Gautier stood up as a waiter brought another chair to the table and she sat down facing him.

'Have you come to Dijon to collect Bishop Arkwright?'

'You are not a very good judge of character, are you, Inspector?'

'Why do you say that?'

'When Bishop Arkwright reaches the Hôtel Cheltenham, which he should do quite soon, he will find that his bill has already been paid and that waiting for him are his tickets for the liner which sails for New York from Cherbourg tomorrow.'

'You are sending him home?'

'Not at all. I am simply saving him from the problems which he would have faced with the Methodist Church, had he failed to be back in the States to resume his episcopal duties next week. Comments are already being made about his behaviour in the newspapers back home.'

A waiter appeared to take their order and after they had given it, Gautier asked Mrs Barclay, 'And why are you here?'

'You are full of questions, Jean-Paul. Let us just say that the reasons for my visit to Dijon will become apparent in due course. Your policeman's curiosity will have to be satisfied with that for the time being.' Her face wore a smile of innocence, but he knew she was laughing at him. One way of escape, he decided, would be to get her to talk about herself.

'Tell me about your life in America,' he said. 'You live in New York, I understand.'

'Coward!' she mocked him, but then added, 'Not in New York but in Long Island ever since my husband died eight years ago. Before that in a suburb of Detroit. Hardly my favourite city, but my husband provided us with a life which allowed us to forget its squalor.'

'His business was successful then?'

'Very.' Her husband, she told him, had been an engineer by training and had invented a technique by which automobiles could be made more rapidly and in greater numbers. He had sold his invention to the big American automobile manufacturers for a sum which enabled him and his wife to live in comfort for the remainder of their lives.

'Poor Henry!' she concluded. 'He did not live very long to enjoy the fruits of his brilliance.'

'Did your support of the temperance movement ever bring you in contact with a Madame Harrington?' Gautier tossed the question at her, expecting nothing.

'Betsy Harrington? I know her well. She also has a home in Long Island. Don't tell me she has fallen foul of the law here!'

'Not at all. She had the misfortune to meet a confidence trickster in Paris.'

'A charming young man, I suppose.'

'Younger than she, I understand.'

'Poor Betsy! She has a weakness for young men.' Mrs Barclay looked at Gautier and smiled, 'I on the other hand, have always preferred more mature lovers.'

Gautier could not decide whether she was teasing him or whether her remark was deliberately provocative. Her sudden arrival in Dijon and the fact that she had taken the trouble to find out his Christian name, had made him wonder.

'How long is it since you saw Madame Harrington?' he asked her.

'We met shortly after she returned from Paris. That would be a month or two ago.'

'Did she mention that she had been a victim of a confidence trick?'

'Never. She would be too proud to admit it if she had been. But I have to say she was in a very bad mood for someone who had just enjoyed a trip to Europe.'

'Do you know where she was staying when she was in Paris?'

'The Ritz, I would think. Betsy always aims for the best.'

'Did she take her own bishop with her?' Gautier asked, teasing.

'Be careful now, Jean-Paul!' Mrs Barclay reached across the table, trying to smack his fingers. 'You don't know me well enough to be impertinent; not yet anyway.'

The confidence trick that had been played on Betsy Harrington made Gautier curious, even though he realized that it had been the fault of her own stupidity or vanity. Wealthy foreign visitors and even rich old French ladies were often succumbing to the wiles of plausible swindlers in Paris, but surely it could not be just coincidence that this particular case seemed to be connected, however remotely with a brutal murder.

He did not allow himself to brood over the matter, but relaxed and enjoyed Deborah Barclay's company. She was a lively dinner companion, telling him amusing stories and teasing him without malice. In due course he would find out her reasons for coming to Dijon and seeking him out, but at that moment they did not seem to matter and he was confident he would be able to deal with them.

When they had finished dinner, they went for a stroll in the streets around the hotel. Like himself Deborah found the old town around the Cathedral of St Benigne fascinating, with its sense of history and charming architecture.

She seemed in a receptive mood, so he decided to ask a question which he had wanted to ask her for some time.

'On the evening when Stephanie Winstock was murdered, you went out to dinner while Bishop Arkwright was at a Methodist meeting. Were you by any chance dining with Philippe Gambon?'

'How did you know that?'

'I guessed.'

'Why? Are you jealous?'

Gautier smiled. 'Should I be?'

'Certainly not. As I told you, I prefer older men.'

She took his arm and smiled at him flirtatiously. Gautier sensed that it had been a mistake to question her. He would have liked to ask her more questions about Philippe, but he decided not to ask them until she was in a more receptive mood. There would be other opportunities, he was sure. When they returned to the hotel they were given the keys to their rooms by the concierge and he escorted her to the second floor.

'Do you know I have been given the same room as I had on my

last visit,' Deborah said as they were going up the stairs. 'Don't you find that ironic?'

'In a way, I suppose.'

They reached the room. She opened the door and stood looking up at him. 'If you were to come in,' she said, 'there would be no need for me to lie, would there?'

There was no ambiguity in the invitation, nor in the smile which accompanied it. Suddenly Gautier knew that he was tempted, but still he hesitated. One reason for his hesitation was conscience. If he accepted the invitation would that mean he was being unfaithful to Ingrid? He dismissed the idea as absurd, as he knew Ingrid would. Another reason was doubt. Deborah Barclay was a good-looking woman, but at no time during the evening, until the last few moments, had he been aware of being physically attracted by her. If he gave way to temptation now would he be just taking advantage of the loneliness of a middle-aged woman?

She was still looking at him. Seeing his hesitation, she reached up, caught the lapel of his coat and pulled him gently into the room.

14

When Gautier arrived there the following morning, the room in which Judge Jolivet was holding the *instruction* was already almost full, but he could not see the Prefect of Police. Although it was no concern of his, he was curious to know where the Prefect was staying. Since at one time Dijon had been his home, he probably still had friends in the city and Gautier felt it was unlikely that he had spent the night at Château Perdrix, in case that would draw attention to himself and might even be seen as in some way compromising the legal proceedings. He still had not arrived in the room when Judge Jolivet opened the day's examination.

The first witnesses of the day seemed to have been chosen almost at random from the many people who might have spoken to Michael O'Flynn in the hours before his death. Some had attended the banquet at the Château Perdrix, either as officers of the new order or simply as guests. None of them seemed able to say anything which might have had a bearing on why O'Flynn had been murdered and Gautier was beginning to form the impression that the *instruction* was losing its impetus.

As he listened to what was being said, he found himself thinking of Deborah Barclay and the last hours they had spent together. Once they were alone in her room the hesitations and doubts he had felt had quickly vanished. She had made love eagerly, but at the same time unselfishly, trying to arouse and satisfy his passion. When in the early hours of the morning he told her that he must leave, she did not try to persuade him to stay, but he could sense the conflicting emotions she was feeling, but which she was mature enough to suppress. There would be time enough for the two of them to explore and release those emotions, for he was sure that had not been the last time they would make love.

At the end of the morning, when the examination was adjourned, he returned to the Hostellerie du Chapeau Rouge, thinking he might find Deborah there and that they might lunch together, but he was told that she had gone shopping in Dijon. Rather than lunch alone in the hotel, he decided he would eat at the Café Le Jaquot. As he was sipping his apéritif in the café, he found himself thinking again of Deborah. When he had put on his clothes and was leaving her room early that morning, she had gone with him, still naked, as far as the door. He could still see her body, slim, the breasts firm, astonishingly seductive for a woman of her age. In America, he had heard, beauty treatments had been developed that could prolong a woman's youth and if that were true, Deborah must have taken full advantage of them.

He put such thoughts out of his mind, conscious that they were a symptom of boredom and instead asked himself what he was doing in Dijon. His place was in Paris, disentangling the last, twisted leads to the solution of Stephanie Winstock's murder. He was still reproaching himself for not being there, when the Prefect of Police came into the café and sat down opposite him.

'I thought I might find you here, Gautier,' he said. 'What happened at the examination this morning?'

'Nothing of any consequence, Monsieur.'

'I had expected that would be so, which was why I did not attend.'

'What will be the outcome? This is no criticism of him, but Judge Jolivet appears to be making little progress.'

'He will have no option but to adjourn the proceedings *sine die*, allowing the police to search for more evidence. I expect that might happen this afternoon, or tomorrow morning at the latest.'

'If it does end this afternoon should I return to Paris?'

'Not yet. You are expected at the wake for Michael O'Flynn this evening.'

'Who will be at the wake?'

'His family, a great many of his friends and no doubt a number of his enemies who feel obliged to go, if only to show that they are not glad he is dead.'

The remark was typical of the Prefect. Gautier knew the man was not cynical, but he had a way of making comments which sounded aggressive and clever, but which when analysed showed that by an unconventional thought process, he had arrived at a conclusion that was perfectly logical.

'Since the wake is not a purely family occasion, would it be possible for me to bring a guest this evening?' The idea had suddenly come to Gautier.

'Who had you in mind? That handsome American matron who was dining with you last evening?'

Gautier knew better than to show that he was surprised. Experience had taught him that the Prefect had an uncanny knack of knowing the movements of all those who worked for him. Even so he felt he should resent the description of Deborah Barclay. Matron was for most people a pejorative term, carrying implications of a staid, charmless dignity which certainly did not apply to Deborah. He knew though that even if the Prefect was teasing him, there would be no malice in it.

'By all means bring Madame Barclay.' The Prefect smiled. 'Like many Americans she may well have Irish blood in her and in that case she should be able to make an interesting contribution to the wake.'

Back at the hotel in the middle of the afternoon session of the *instruction*, Gautier received a message from the hotel's office telling him that the Sûreté in Paris had been trying to reach him by telephone. He guessed that the call must have come from Surat and would be a response to the telegram he had sent him the previous afternoon. He left the room, found one of the hotel's telephones and began putting a call through to Sûreté headquarters.

The telephone was relatively new in France and the network still primitive. When making a call one had to rely on the goodwill and efficiency of the telephone operator and this put operators in a dominant position, which many of them found hard to resist. As a result telephonists had become a powerful clique, exercising their might with a dictatorial arrogance. Gautier had learnt to live with this when making calls in Paris, but making an inter-urban call was a new and intimidating experience. He was eventually connected to the Sûreté in Paris, but the connection was broken more than once and he needed to make several attempts before his call to Surat was completed.

From it he learnt that Parker had confirmed that the body discovered earlier in the week had in fact been that of Crozier. The dead man had been married and his widow had been traced. She had been distressed, but not greatly surprised to hear that he was dead. He had often told her, she said, that his *métier* was a secret and a dangerous one and he would often be absent from home for several days. He had left her well provided for and had recently brought home large sums in cash which he kept hidden in their apartment. She knew little of what he was doing, apart from the fact that he had left his job at the detective agency for more lucrative employment. He had not mentioned the names of his contacts and she knew only that over the past week a Monsieur Delarue had left messages for him on several occasions.

'When was Crozier murdered?' Gautier asked Surat.

'We do not know for certain but at least two and perhaps even three days ago. He was shot in an alley and his body was hidden among the junk and rubbish that accumulates in such places.'

After completing his telephone call, Gautier was crossing the hotel's vestibule on his way back to Judge Jolivet's examination, when he saw Deborah Barclay. She seemed to be in good spirits and looked younger than ever as she came over to him.

'Will I be seeing you this evening, Jean-Paul?' she asked him.

'I very much hope so. You and I have been invited to a vigil this evening.'

'A vigil?'

'It is an Irish ceremony. In Ireland they call it a wake.'

'A wake? I once went to a wake held in Boston by some friends of my husband. Everyone drank too much, but even so it was entertaining.'

'Then you will come with me?'

'I would not miss it for the world!'

They agreed that he would contact her again as soon as he knew more about the arrangements for the wake and Gautier returned to the room in which the *instruction* was being held. He sat there as more witnesses were being questioned by the judge, but he was not really listening to what was being said. An idea was forming in his mind and there were calculations to be done. In a notebook that he was carrying he began jotting down the dates and times when different events occurred over the past two weeks.

Clearly the most important dates were those of the three murders; of Michael O'Flynn, of Stephanie Winstock and now of Crozier. From what Surat had told him Crozier must have been shot either on the day when he and Surat had visited the Wilmington Detective Agency or the previous day. Since he had been shot one might assume that he had been killed at night, or at least in the evening, for discharging a firearm during daylight would draw attention to the assassin. Gautier was inclined to believe that Crozier must have been shot during the evening prior to his and Surat's visit to the detective agency, which would have been the evening of the wine-tasting.

Looking back he could see other incidents which seemed to play a part in the theory he was trying to construct. One was the banquet at the Château Perdrix, another was the wine-tasting at the Salle Delacroix and a third was the fracas which Pauline Fenn had caused at the Hôtel Trumpington. There were others, seemingly trivial, which might help to provide a time-frame against which his theory might be tested, like for example his meeting with Lucien Gambon and his son André at the railway station in Dijon and even the lunch given by Madame Pitot the baker's wife.

He had filled up three pages of his notebook, but was no nearer reaching any conclusions when Judge Jolivet brought the afternoon session of the examination to a close. The Prefect of Police was nowhere to be seen, so Gautier decided that he should go and consult the hotel's concierge on how transport might be arranged to take Deborah Barclay and himself to the Château Perdrix for the wake. When he reached the conciergerie he found that another guest was making the same enquiry. He was only mildly surprised when he saw that the guest was Duthrey.

'I did not expect to see you here, old friend,' he said.

'Nor I you,' Duthey replied.

'Let me guess. You have been invited to the wake for Michael O'Flynn.'

'I have and between you and me I am not sure that I should have accepted the invitation. For one thing it is a long way to come to attend a ceremony which, they tell me, borders on the irreligious. And now that I have made the journey, I discover that my room at the hotel is not ready.'

Because of the interest aroused in and around Dijon by the murder of Michael O'Flynn, all the hotels in the town were busy and it had needed the influence of important people to secure Duthrey a room for the night in the Hostellerie du Chapeau Rouge. Even then he had been obliged to accept one which had only been vacated that afternoon. Gautier knew that all his married life Duthrey had been pampered by his wife, never allowed to suffer the smallest inconvenience and that he became bad tempered whenever his wishes were frustrated.

'Instead of waiting for your room,' he suggested, 'why do we not go and take a glass at a nearby café? There are matters on which I need your opinion.'

'In that case, by all means let us go.'

They left Duthrey's valise with the concierge, went out of the hotel and walked until they found a quiet, unpretentious café. Gautier deliberately did not choose the Café Le Jaquot for there was always a chance that the Prefect might be there. Telling Duthrey that there were matters on which he wished to have his opinion had not been just an invention to soften his irritation. When collecting information for his book on the wines of Burgundy, Duthrey had spent many hours on research. He had studied not only the historical development in techniques of vinification, but also the background of the main families in the region.

'Tell me,' he said when they were sitting in the café with an open bottle of wine between them, 'what do you know of Joséphine O'Flynn? Before she married she was a Dubois, I understand.'

'She was; the only daughter of old Auguste Dubois. whose family owned what had once been the best-known vineyard in the Côtes de Nuits. People used to describe him as the grandfather of Burgundy wine.'

'You are speaking of him in the past.'

'I am and not only because he is dead. In the last years of his life his family's wine is said to have fallen from the very high standards it had maintained for generations.'

'Was there any reason for that?'

Duthrey shrugged. 'Different people will advance different reasons. One may have been that his only son was killed in the war with Prussia. He was left with only his daughter who was some years younger than his son, but people say he never got over the loss and from then on he slipped into melancholy. He neglected the vineyard, the business went downhill rapidly and just before he died he was obliged to sell it.'

'Who bought it? Michael O'Flynn?'

'You cannot stop playing the detective, can you, Gautier?' Duthrey smiled. 'No, Dubois's vineyard was purchased by a consortium of local businessmen. It is their intention to invest capital in the company, to restore it to a stable position and, once it is a viable concern, to sell it to a suitable purchaser who can be relied on to conform to the best traditions of the Burgundy wine trade.'

'Who would that be? Lucien Gambon perhaps?'

'You are incorrigible, Gautier!'

'But at least Dubois was able to arrange a good marriage for his daughter.'

'Not all that good. You see he was unable to provide her with a dowry.'

Although he had never had any daughters nor even a sister, Gautier understood the importance of the dowry in French family life. Being married without a dowry would be a badge of shame that a girl would have to carry with her all her days. It would also, unless her husband was unusually tolerant, weaken her position in the marriage. Perhaps that was the reason for the expression of discontent he had noticed in Joséphine O'Flynn's face.

'I have the impression that the O'Flynns' marriage was not a happy one,' Gautier said.

'Who told you that?' Duthrey asked him sharply.

'No one has ever discussed the matter with me. It was an opinion I had formed. Madame O'Flynn did not exactly strike one as the grieving widow when she was being examined by Judge Jolivet.'

'People are always ready to denigrate Joséphine, but she deserves sympathy. Michael O'Flynn was an autocratic husband, very much in the Irish tradition.'

Gautier could sense where Duthrey's loyalties lay, so he decided it would be tactful to say no more about Joséphine O'Flynn.

'It is not only the Irish who are autocratic,' he remarked. 'Lucien Gambon appears to be autocratic and typically French in his attitude towards his family.'

'That is true. Even when his wife was alive it was always Gambon who insisted on family discipline. He is often needlessly severe with his two sons.'

'André certainly appears to be overawed by his father.'

'There is some truth in that. He is the elder son and Lucien expects too much of him.'

'In what way?'

Duthrey explained that Lucien Gambon intended that André would inherit the family business. He had also bought him a small vineyard near Beaune and expected that he would build this up by mergers and purchases until it became one of the leading producers in the region. Sacrifices had been made for that ambition. André, as the elder son, had been given exemption from military service and had been made to live a hard life in a rural community, while his brother after military service had been sent to Paris, where he enjoyed the freedom of a lively social life.

'Freedom?' Gautier said. 'His father was furious when Philippe failed to attend the wine-tasting earlier this week. André was even sent to my office to apologize to me.'

'One can understand that. Philippe gave no warning that he would not be there and his excuse for failing to attend was palpably false.'

'People say that at one time André and Philippe would have liked to marry O'Flynn's daughters, but that O'Flynn would not allow it.'

'O'Flynn?' Duthrey exclaimed. 'It was Gambon who opposed the idea! He did not believe that the girls were a good enough match for his precious sons.'

'Then who does he have in mind as wives for them?'

'You had better ask him yourself. For I understand that Madame O'Flynn has very surprisingly invited all three of the Gambons to the wake tonight.'

15

The wake for Michael O'Flynn was being held in two rooms at the Château Perdrix. At one end of the larger of the two rooms hung a portrait of O'Flynn, which must have been painted only a short time previously, for in it he was wearing the scarlet robes and gold sash of a Chevalier of the *Confrérie du Tastevin de Bourgogne*. Beneath the portrait stood a coffin covered with white flowers; the walls of the room, which was lit only by clusters of candles, were decorated with drapes of green silk. As the guests arrived they were led up to the coffin by Joséphine O'Flynn or one of her daughters, so they could pay their respects to the dead man. Most of the guests seemed uncertain of what form their respects should take. Some crossed themselves, others simply stood by the coffin with their heads bowed, two elderly ladies – aunts perhaps or cousins – even knelt and seemed to be offering a brief prayer.

Mrs Barclay and Gautier, together with Duthrey, had been driven from Dijon to the château in an automobile, the latest De Dion Bouton model powered by a petroleum engine, one of a fleet of autos which had been engaged to bring those who lived any distance from the château to the wake. They were among the first guests to arrive and, after filing past the coffin, they went to the smaller of the two rooms where the refreshments for the evening were waiting.

The staff of the château stood ready behind long tables which were laden with food, but Gautier, who had once visited Dublin and knew the reputation of the Irish for conviviality, was not surprised to see that the accent of the hospitality was to be on drink. Not only the product of the Château Perdrix, but a whole range of red and white wines from every part of Burgundy were on offer to the guests. At one end of the room stood a large barrel, from which a man dressed in knee-breeches and a velvet waistcoat was waiting to fill glass tankards with stout.

When they stood with glasses of wine in their hands, Mrs Barclay remarked, 'I must say that I was not expecting that Michael O'Flynn would be with us this evening. Is that not rather macabre?'

'Do not concern yourself,' Duthrey said, 'the coffin is empty. O'Flynn was buried as soon as the police had satisfied themselves on the cause of his death. The coffin is symbolic, just a focal point for the celebration of his life.'

The three of them had been among the first of the guests to arrive and Gautier had noticed that the Prefect of Police was already there. He found himself wondering whether he was staying at the château and if so, for how much longer he would remain. As far as one knew there was no urgent reason for him to return to Paris. A short time ago Gautier himself would have been anxious to get back to the Sûreté, and apply himself to solving the murder of Stephanie Winstock. That was when he believed there was no possible connection between her death and that of Michael O'Flynn. Now he had decided that the two were linked and that their solution was to be found in Dijon.

When Mrs Barclay had removed her wrap, he had seen that she was wearing a white dress trimmed with green and decorated with bows tied in the form of shamrocks. Choosing to wear it had been a bold decision, for one might have expected that more sombre and even funereal colours might have been expected of ladies attending a solemn occasion. As it was, her clothes and her demeanour appeared to blend perfectly with the mood of their hostess and her two daughters. Gautier wondered whether this might be because, as the Prefect had suggested, she had Irish blood in her.

On the drive from Dijon, she had been telling Duthrey and himself about her life in America. From what she had said and her answers to a few questions which he had adroitly slipped into the conversation, he had decided that she was younger than he had at first supposed. In all probability she was not much more than two or three years older than he was. He found the thought reassuring and then immediately reproached himself for his vanity. Making love with an older woman was not a matter for shame.

As the two rooms began to fill up, Gautier recognized several of the other guests as they were received by Joséphine O'Flynn and her two daughters. Judge Jolivet was among them and so were Inspector Le Harivel and Armand Pascal. The Gambons arrived together and one could sense a sympathetic tenderness in the old man's manner towards Joséphine, as he grasped her hand and allowed his lips to linger over it.

After a time the Prefect of Police came over to join Mrs Barclay, Duthrey and Gautier.

'Are you enjoying this Irish occasion?' he asked them.

'Of course,' Duthrey replied, 'but are there to be no formal ceremonies, no speeches?'

'To be frank I am not absolutely certain of what is meant to happen and I am not sure our hostess is either.'

'Are there no Irish here to guide us?' Gautier asked.

'Not as far as I know. There is no Irish blood remaining in the

O'Flynn family, not even through distant cousins. Madame O'Flynn is holding the wake only because in his will her husband asked that there should be one. As I understand it, the formal part of the evening will start with an address by the Catholic bishop. There may also be Irish singing.'

'Songs of mourning no doubt,' Duthrey suggested.

'Some may be sad, but you can be sure they will all be sentimental and typically Irish.'

'And after the homily?'

'I am told by those who know that wakes in Ireland seldom have any formal structure. Their success relies on the mood of those attending, on inspiration if you like. Anyone is free to speak or to sing and frequently many do, especially if the drink is flowing freely.'

'Let us hope that this evening holds no unpleasant surprises,' Duthrey said sententiously.

'It may well do,' the Prefect said, 'and I would not put it past Gautier to supply one.'

As the Prefect was speaking everyone was being asked to move into the room in which the coffin lay. 'If I were you,' he advised the others, 'I would make sure your glasses are full.'

'Why?' Mrs Barclay asked him. 'Will there be toasts?'

'Very possibly, but in any event the bishop is not noted for brevity.'

The Prefect had been right when he suggested that the opening address at the wake might become tedious. The sentiments expressed by the bishop were admirable and much of what he said might well have been true. By the standards of the Church, Michael O'Flynn might well have been a devoted husband and caring father, a fair employer and a generous supporter of good causes, but after a time the restlessness of his audience suggested that they would have preferred not to have been obliged to hear the bishop extolling these virtues at such length.

As he was listening, Gautier was thinking of the remark which the Prefect had just made about surprises. He had found more than once in the past that the man had a disconcerting ability to sense what Gautier was thinking and even to anticipate what he intended to do. At other times he appeared, by seemingly casual remarks, to be steering Gautier towards a course of action which he felt was needed.

In the closing passage of his speech the bishop denounced O'Flynn's murderer.

'Let us hope,' he said, 'that whoever struck down this husband, this father, this servant of the Church, is speedily brought to justice.'

Another speaker, the chief steward of the Château Perdrix, took his place, standing in front of the coffin. As the man paid a more simple but sincere tribute to his former master, Gautier found himself wondering whether this might be the moment for him to act. He was reasonably confident that he knew what had happened and the names of those involved in O'Flynn's death. Even so there was one more piece of speculation which he would like to have had confirmed so he could present the conclusions which he had reached with convincing logic.

Presently many of the guests at the wake began drifting back into the other room, where they had their glasses refilled or sampled the pies and cakes which had been laid out for them. Gautier and Deborah Barclay went with them.

'Tell me,' he said to her on the way, 'when you dined with Philippe Gambon did you discuss Betsy Harrington?'

'No, why should we have?'

'I just wondered whether you might have.'

Deborah frowned, trying to remember. 'Now I come to think

of it, her name was mentioned, but only casually. Philippe simply asked me if I knew her, nothing more.' She looked at Gautier, smiling. 'I believe you are jealous of him, Jean-Paul.'

He did not bother to deny her accusation. 'As you may have noticed, both the Gambon brothers are here tonight.'

Deborah looked round the room, screwing up her eyes and peering. It was the first time that Gautier realized she was short-sighted.

'Where are they?'

Gautier pointed out Philippe, who stood opposite them, talking to Cara O'Flynn.

'I can see now that it is Philippe,' she said, 'although I must say he looks different in some way.'

'When you saw him previously he may not have had a beard.'

'You could be right, although surely he could not have grown that beard in so short a time.'

'Beards can be acquired or discarded. Nothing is easier.'

'You are saying his beard is false. Why should he disguise himself?'

'You will find that out, if you will be kind enough to do as I ask. Not now, but at an appropriate moment.'

'I am not sure, Jean-Paul, that I should be trusting you, but I do.'

'What I want you to do is really very simple. Just wait until I tell you.'

He would not say more because he knew she would start asking questions and there would be a time for answering questions later. A few minutes later everyone returned to the room in which the coffin stood and heard more speeches and some maudlin songs, French as well as Irish. Gautier waited until they were over and until he and Deborah were standing in a group which included Joséphine O'Flynn and her daughters, Gambon and his sons, the Prefect of Police and Judge Jolivet. Inspector Le Harivel was also not far away. Then at Gautier's prompting Deborah said what he wanted her to say.

'We have met before, have we not?' she called out to Philippe Gambon. 'Monsieur Paul Delarue, is it not?'

Philippe's reply was very much what Gautier had expected. He looked startled but his hesitation was only momentary.

'We have met before, of course, Madame Barclay, but even so you must be mistaking me for someone else. I know no one of the name of Delarue.'

'Perhaps when Madame last met you, Monsieur,' Gautier said, 'you were using one of your other names. Could it have been Desfontaines? Or perhaps it was Robinet?'

'I have no idea what you are talking about,' Philippe said brusquely.

'No. Of course Robinet was the name you chose for the man who was paid to kill Stephanie Winstock.'

'What in heaven's name is this man saying?' Lucien Gambon complained angrily. Then he said to Gautier, 'Have you gone mad?'

'Let him continue,' the Prefect said. 'I am sure there is a purpose behind his questions.'

'Is he accusing my son of murder?'

'Of complicity in murder,' Gautier replied. 'I do not know whether he killed anyone with his own hand, but he played a part in at least three murders.'

'Which murders?' the Prefect asked.

'Of Michael O'Flynn, Stephanie Winstock and a detective named Crozier.'

Now everyone in the room was staring at Philippe, waiting to hear what he would say.

'As I have already told you,' he said to Gautier. 'I was in

Bordeaux on the night of Monsieur O'Flynn's death.'

'Really? That is strange! Madame O'Flynn told me you were dining in this château with her and her daughters, while your brother claims you were attending a reunion of some of your old army friends.'

Philippe's eyes filled with fear. He did not stop to hear any more, but suddenly turned and made a dash to leave the room. Inspector Le Harivel was standing between him and escape and, reacting as any trained policeman would, he grabbed Philippe as he reached the doorway. Shouting and swearing, Philippe struggled to free himself but two of the château's servants helped Le Harivel to restrain him. The other guests stared, bewildered. Three candles were knocked to the floor and Duthrey moved quickly to stop the carpet being set alight.

'Monsieur le Juge,' the Prefect said to Jolivet. 'May I suggest that you have Gambon detained, at least until Inspector Gautier's accusations can be explored? One of the crimes of which he is being accused falls under your jurisdiction.'

'There are others who should be detained,' Gautier said. 'The murder of Michael O'Flynn was part of a conspiracy.'

'You had better tell us all you know,' the Prefect said. One could see that he knew he would not like what he was going to hear.

'He knows nothing!' Joséphine O'Flynn called out shrilly. 'Can you not see? This is all pure invention!'

'You may say that, Madame,' Gautier said, 'but as the prime mover of the conspiracy, you should certainly be detained.'

'Only the mind of a policeman could have sifted the truth from that imbroglio of falsehoods and crime,' Duthrey said.

He, Deborah Barclay and Gautier were back at the Hostellerie du Chapeau Rouge, where they were taking a last glass of wine to restore their equanimity at the end of what had been a disturbing evening. Duthrey's remark may have sounded like a complaint and in a way he was grumbling, since his admiration for Michael O'Flynn and the comfortable picture he had formed of those around him in the wine business, had been suddenly shattered. At heart though he was loyal to his friend Gautier and had always taken pride in the success with which he had solved many notorious criminal cases.

As they were being driven back to the hotel from the Château Perdrix, Gautier had filled in for them the details of what he had told the guests at the wake. He had explained how Joséphine O'Flynn, longing to be free of her husband and of the life she was leading in the provinces, had persuaded the two Gambon brothers that he should be murdered. Their reward was that they would then marry Cara and Bronagh, who would come to marriage with extravagantly generous dowries made possible by the sale of the château and its vineyards. The brothers, seeing at last an opportunity to escape from their dependence on an autocratic father, had not been difficult to persuade. In any case Philippe had a criminal's mind, for he was already trying to free himself by swindling money out of wealthy old ladies.

'The murder would have been relatively simple to arrange,' Gautier explained, 'as Joséphine would have known what the movements of her husband would be on that evening. She may even have telephoned the hotel to find out where his room was situated. Philippe, or it may have been André, concealed somewhere would have been waiting for him to return and O'Flynn would have opened the door to his knock. I tend to believe it was probably Philippe, for after serving in the army he would know how to handle a weapon and how to kill quickly and quietly.'

Duthrey shook his head sadly. 'You make it sound so simple. What went wrong?'

'Nothing. They might well have got away with the murder, for no one would have suspected the three of them. Like many conspirators they could not believe their luck and that made them nervous. First Philippe, then Madame O'Flynn and finally André tried to find out from me how much the police knew. Foolishly, for at that point the Sûreté was not even involved.'

'How did you come to be involved?' Deborah asked.

'You may find that this sounds ridiculous, but the two crimes merged purely by chance. The decision of an English milady, Lady Jane Shelford, to meet her American friend in Paris triggered off a series of misunderstandings and two murders which became linked with the death of O'Flynn.'

Gautier told them that Philippe Gambon had made a point of choosing as victims for his confidence tricks middle-aged English or American ladies, who were not only susceptible to his charm, but who were on rare visits to Paris. Because they would not be returning for several months, even years, they would not be in a position to expose him, even when they realized they had been duped. Then at quite short notice, Lady Jane had been persuaded by Stephanie Winstock to make a second visit, so that they would meet in Paris for her annual holiday, instead of on her estate in England.

'That need not have mattered,' Gautier said. 'Philippe could easily have managed to avoid meeting Lady Jane for the short time she was to be in Paris. But there were complications. One was that a vindictive American, Mrs Harrington, had employed a detective agency to discover who had swindled her.'

Gautier explained that Crozier, one of the detectives employed by the agency, had discovered that Philippe Gambon was the swindler. He must have tried to blackmail Philippe, telling him that he had orders to give his name to Stephanie Winstock when she arrived in Paris. Philippe dealt with that threat skilfully by offering Crozier a much larger sum of money if he killed Winstock. Crozier agreed.

'What followed might be called a comedy of errors,' Gautier said, 'except that violent crime is never comic. Another complicating factor was that Pauline Fenn went to the Hôtel Trumpington posing as Stephanie Winstock. When he went to the hotel to meet his father, Philippe, who had never met Winstock, must have heard Fenn claiming to be her and to say that she was staying at the Pension Beau Séjour. He told Crozier, who booked in at the pension under the name of Robinet and killed the first woman he found in their room, who as it happened *was* Stephanie Winstock. So one might say that in a way, Mademoiselle Winstock was murdered by accident.'

'Poor woman,' Duthrey said. 'We were ready to condemn her for trying to foist her childish beliefs on us, but she did not deserve to be murdered.'

'In a way without meaning to be,' Gautier told him, 'I was instrumental in bringing matters to a head, when I named Lady Jane as the guest I would be taking to the wine tasting. Philippe knew then that he could not go to the tasting and, feeling that a net was closing around him, he panicked. It must have been that night that he decided he could not trust Crozier and must silence him. He arranged that they should meet and then killed him.'

By that time all the three conspirators thought that Gautier knew more than he did. They then began lying, inventing stories to prove that none of them had been involved in O'Flynn's murder. Philippe Gambon had already told Gautier that he was in Bordeaux, André invented another story and Joséphine invented a different one.

'And then as with all criminals,' Duthrey said, rather pompously Gautier thought, 'once you struck at their weakness, their courage collapsed. I can see them all now in the prison of La

Roquette, setting out on that early morning walk to the guillotine.'

'It seemed to me,' Deborah Barclay said, 'that your friend Monsieur Duthrey did not give you enough credit for bringing the murderers of O'Flynn to justice.'

'Poor Duthrey! The evening has been painful for him. He had a high regard for O'Flynn and has always been a fervent defender of family virtues.'

'When did you first begin to suspect that there had been a conspiracy to murder Michael O'Flynn?'

'Late; far too late really,' Gautier replied. 'I thought it odd when Philippe came to see me soon after O'Flynn's murder, but it was not until André gave me a needlessly long and complicated story of why Philippe had not been at the wine tasting, that I began to wonder whether the three of them had been in league.'

He might also have told Deborah that it was even later, when she told him that Philippe had taken her out to dinner, that the seemingly disparate elements of the speculative theory he was forming began falling into place. Why should André have invented a story of a military reunion on the night of Stephanie Winstock's murder? Clearly he could not have known that Philippe did not need an alibi that evening, since he had been dining with Deborah Barclay. So, if the brothers and Joséphine O'Flynn had been in league, in their panic they were not consulting each other on the stories they were telling. It was this that made him decide to take a chance and float his theory of the murders at the wake. His immediate success had surprised him.

He did not tell Deborah all this for by then they were making their way upstairs. Duthrey had left them, grumbling at the lateness of the hour, for unlike many journalists, he was not a man for late-night carousing, but liked to go to his bed early. Gautier sensed that another motive for his leaving them may have been tact. He said no more about the murders, for he sensed that she had other things on her mind.

To prove him right she suddenly laughed and squeezed his arm. 'I hope I will not have to pull you into my room again tonight,' she said.

'If you leave me outside, I may well break the door down.'

'Good!' When they were inside the room and alone, she turned to face him. 'May I ask you a favour, Jean-Paul?'

'Of course.'

'Then will you seduce me tonight? Just this once?' She looked up at him and when she saw he was not laughing at her, went on, 'I know it will sound absurd, but women of my age are never seduced. It is we who have to do the seducing. I want to remember what it is like, to feel the delicious sensation of yielding.'

Gautier could see that she was being serious and he found her request oddly moving. So he did as she asked, using the techniques of persuasion he might have used on a girl of eighteen. She responded to his caresses, reluctantly at first, pushing his fingers away as they explored her body and then unable to restrain little cries of delight. Finally, when she was almost naked, he picked her up as she still put on a pretence of a struggle and carried her to the bed.

Their love-making was even more intense than it had been the previous night. When it was over, she said nothing but he could feel the emotion in her.

'How much longer will you be in France?' he asked her.

'I am due to sail one week from today.'

'Then we have six nights left. And you will be coming back of course?'

She put a finger on his lips. 'Don't talk about the future, Jean-Paul. Everyone knows it brings bad luck.'

'Surely Americans are not superstitious?'

'Look at it this way. You have helped me recapture my youth, given me what in America we would call a marvellous Indian summer. I will treasure the memory of it, but I realize it cannot last.'

'With your passionate spirit and your wonderful, seductive body you have years of love left in you.'

'My husband always thought in engineering terms. He too admired my body, but he used to say it was a wasting asset.'

Gautier reached out and pulled her to him. 'In that case, why don't we stop wasting it?'